MR. CHICKEE'S MESSY MISSION

MR. CHICKEE'S MESSY MISSION

CHRISTOPHER PAUL CURTIS

WENDY
LAMB
BOOKS

Published by Wendy Lamb Books
an imprint of Random House Children's Books
a division of Random House, Inc.
New York

www.randomhouse.com/kids

Educators and librarians, for a variety of teaching tools, visit us at
www.randomhouse.com/teachers.

Library of Congress Cataloging-in-Publication Data

Curtis, Christopher Paul.
Mr. Chickee's Messy Mission / Christopher Paul Curtis.
p. cm.
Summary: Flint Future Detective Club members Steve Carter and his friends Russell and
Richelle follow Russell's dog, Rodney Rodent, into a mural to chase a demonic-looking
gnome, only to find the mysterious Mr. Chickee on the other side.
ISBN-13: 978-0-385-32775-6 (hardcover) 978-0-385-90942-6 (lib. ed.)
[1. Gnomes—Fiction.   2. Dogs—Fiction.   3. African Americans—Fiction.   4. Flint
(Mich.)—Fiction.   5. Mystery and detective stories.]   I. Title.   II. Title: Mister Chickee's
Messy Mission.
PZ7.C94137Mrg 2007
[Fic]—dc22
2006026690

Printed in the United States of America

10 9 8 7 6 5 4 3 2 1

First Edition

Dedicated to the Pediatric R.E.A.D. (Reading Early
Accelerates Development) Program Committee

Kaysandra Curtis
Lynn Guest
Kristi Stearns
Elaine Astles
Mike Wilcox
Nancy Nosanchuk
Lois Smedick
Jean Foster
Virginia Allibon Kampe
The Grade 5 students of Hetherington Elementary School
Lily and Emma Collins

Asante Sana to Daniel M. Mungai
for his help with the Swahili

ONE

Chance of Snow: 100%!
or
John Henry Was a Steel-Drivin' Man!

STEVEN DAEMON CARTER THOUGHT there was about a 75% chance that it was his name that was being called. But he'd learned before that that wasn't quite high enough. It wasn't worth going through all the trouble of waking yourself up and answering unless you were somewhere around 88 to 90% sure that some annoying parent was trying to ruin another good night's sleep.

A few seconds later he was about 85.2% sure that his father was calling him. Close, but no cigar. But 85.2% *was* the level when Steven would start grumbling about having a good dream interrupted and would begin pulling sheets and pillows and covers over his ears.

"STEVEN DAEMON CARTER!"

Now, that was 100%!

All sleep and all grumbling and all dreams and pretty much all sheet and pillow pulling came to a dead stop.

"Yes, Dad?"

"Are you up?"

"Really," Steven thought, "what kind of a question is that? Does he think Zoopy has learned how to talk? Does he think . . ."

"STE-E-VEN!"

"Yes, Dad! I'm up!"

"No! Get up *now*!"

Steven and his father had different definitions of the word *up*. In Dad's eyes *up* meant Steven had cleaned his room . . . okay, okay, had cleaned his room by shoving things under his bed, had brushed his teeth . . . all right, all right, had *thought* about brushing his teeth, had washed his face . . . I know, I know, had wet at least one of his fingers to wipe the gray, lumpy gunk out of the corners of his eyes, was dressed and was anxiously standing in his doorway waiting to do whatever Dad wanted him to do.

In Steven's eyes *up* was being awake enough to know he needed another two or three hours' sleep.

But as Dad loved saying to his son, "When *you* start paying the rent around here, *you* can start saying what definitions are."

Steven squinched his left eye shut, pulled the pillow from his face and got ready to let the morning's brightness come into his right eye. Only problem was when he opened his right eye, it saw nothing but darkness.

"I can't believe it! It's still dark outside! How early is he getting me up this time?"

His right eye looked at the alarm clock. What it saw was so shocking that he had to unsquinch his left eye to make sure this was real.

It was. The red numbers glared 4:21 a.m.!

Now Steven was *really* up!

"D-a-a-a-d! Do you know what time it is?" he yelled from under his pillow.

"Ste-e-e-ven! Have you looked outside?"

Dad was doing it again! He would never allow his son to answer a question with a question, but he sure liked doing it himself.

Steven clomped to his window and pulled the curtain aside. It was unbelievable! This was the eighth time in two weeks that exactly two feet of snow had covered everything outside. Everything, that is, in the Carters' yard and their two next-door neighbors' yards. The odd thing was, once again, it looked like these were the only houses in the neighborhood that had more than just a coating of snow on them.

An even odder thing was that that same confused Canada goose was flying circles around the house again. Every time they got one of these weird snowstorms, this weird goose would show up too.

"Hmmm," he said, watching the goose, "aren't geese supposed to fly in a V, not an O? Oh, well."

Now, two feet of snow on only three houses and a goose

flying the wrong letter might seem like the kinds of mysteries that Steven, the president of the Flint Future Detectives, might want to investigate. But he couldn't be bothered, he had much more important things on his mind. Things like how could he get even with Dad for getting him up so early. Things like exactly how much longer he was going to be able to stay as president of the Flint Future Detectives. Things like how unfair it was that he was the one who was going to have to go out and shovel. It was bad enough that he had to do his family's sidewalk and porch and driveway, what was worse was that Dad made him go shovel out both neighbors too.

Steven flopped back onto his bed. "Dad, it's too early. I'll do it later."

"Okay, mister! That's it!"

These were never good words to hear from Dad, especially when Steven's room looked like it did now. He jumped up and had half of last week's clothes stuffed under his bed before his bedroom door exploded open.

Dad said, "As of . . ."—he looked at his watch—"four-twenty-two a.m., Friday, November the tenth, you are banned from ever saying 'I'll do it later.' From this day until the time you introduce me to my first grandchild, when you want to say 'I'll do it later,' you will instead sing the first nine words of 'Home on the Range,' after which you will give a good old cowboy 'Yee-haw!', slap the ground twice and scream out, 'Bra-zohs!' "

Dad made him do these weird, embarrassing things to discourage him from being so repetitive.

"Man," Steven thought, "these word-substitute thingies are getting way too complicated. Maybe I *should* make a list of what I say too much and work on not saying the same things over and over."

He was just about to start the list but then thought, "Naah, I'll do it late . . . oops!"

Before he could start singing "Home on the Range," Dad said, "It's time you started showing a little more conscientiousness around here, young man, do you understand?"

Steven thought, "Are you kidding? I bet not even Richelle Cyrus-Herndon knows what that word means, and she's the smartest kid at Clark Elementary School."

He knew better than to tell his father that he had no idea what *conscientiousness* meant. That would cause another trip to look up the word in Great-great-grampa Carter's bad-dispositioned dictionary, something he really wasn't trying to do at any time, especially not at four-something in the morning. Oh yeah, the dictionary would give definitions, but only after it had insulted and disrespected Steven on its copyright page.

"Yes, Dad, I understand."

"Good, put on some mittens, your boots and a hat and get out there and shovel the Millers' driveway and sidewalk, Dr. Taylor's, and finally ours. I've told you a million times that shoveling snow is dangerous for seniors. And I want those sidewalks *clean* too. None of these little paths through the snow, I want to see the edge of the grass on both sides of the sidewalk when you're done. Do you understand?"

"Yes, Dad."

Steven thought, "I understand that that patch of brown skin on the top of your head looks like someone shoveled your hair all the way to the edges, I understand that I wish I had a couple of brothers and sisters so I could say you loved them more than you love me, I understand that if shoveling snow is dangerous for the Millers and Dr. Taylor, then it *must* be dangerous for—"

"STE-E-E-VEN!"

Steven went to wash up. He ran the warm water and stuck his finger under the tap. He dug the eye crud out of the corners of his eyes. He looked in the mirror to see if there were any drool marks to wipe off and if anything had migrated out of his nose overnight; clean on both accounts. That took care of face washing, next step teeth brushing.

AN IMPORTANT WORD FROM WALPOLE ISLAND'S BEST DENTIST, DR. JULIE FRANCES JONES!

Ninety-nine point seven percent of the dentists in the United States, Canada, Mexico, the continents of Africa, South America, Asia, and Europe, the Caribbean, Micronesia, the north side of Flint and two counties in England have declared that Steven Daemon Carter's dental-care techniques are hideous and should not be imitated. Dr. Julie Frances Jones of Walpole Island, Ontario, states, "This kid is so nasty and unhygienic that folks will soon be calling him

Gummy, because if he keeps this up, he won't have a tooth left in his head by the time he's fifteen years old."

Here's what Steven did, which is exactly what you *shouldn't* do:

He cupped his left hand and put it over his mouth and nose, then blew so that he could get a good whiff of his breath. His eyes didn't water and the room didn't start spinning around, so he said, "Ahhh, fresh as morning dew!"

He rewet his finger and ran it over each of his teeth . . . well, the front two anyway.

"I know it's a lot of work," he said, looking into the mirror and giving a movie-star smile, "but taking care of your teeth is very important!"

He washed and dried his hands and headed back to the bedroom.

AN OPPOSING WORD FROM GREAT-GREAT-GRAMPA CARTER'S DICTIONARY

Please don't listen to Dr. Jones. Following Steven's dental-care plan leads to many exciting words being included in my pages. Look up the following: *gingivitis, toothlessness, loneliness, ostracism, root canal, plaque, halitosis* and my favorite, that delightfully pungent aroma that is two steps worse than halitosis: *funkatosis*!

Steven rummaged under his bed for his mittens and hat, then pulled on his boots. Sighing heavily, he grabbed the shovel and headed outside.

"Man," he thought as he stood on his porch and looked at the twenty-four inches of snow in his yard, "it just isn't fair. Why is it that for the eighth time this month there's hardly any snow across the street or down the block? The weather forecaster said there were only going to be light flurries, but these three yards have been buried! It just isn't fair."

Steven paused to figure which of his neighbors he should do first. There were problems with starting on either one.

The neighbors on the left, the Millers, were the nicest people in the world, but if they heard Steven shoveling, they'd come out and force him back in their house to eat cookies and drink hot chocolate. Not that he had anything against cookies and hot chocolate, but the price he had to pay for these treats just wasn't worth it; he'd have to listen to their long, make-you-want-to-snooze old-timers' stories.

Those dull Tuskegee Airmen tales, and stories about struggling through the Depression, were enough to make him want to voluntarily take one of Dad's punishments.

The neighbor on the right, Dr. Taylor, was worse. She was a retired professor from the University of Michigan–Flint and was about a hundred years old and 101% mean! Mom and Dad said she was "spry." Steven figured that must mean "evil and crabby." He was shocked when Great-great-grampa Carter's dictionary told him it meant "full of life, active, nimble, especially an elderly person."

Mom also called her a "feisty, independent spirit." No matter what the dictionary said, Steven knew that was nothing but a polite way of saying she was a hardheaded grouch.

She hated, hated, *hated* when Steven shoveled her walk! She told him she wasn't so old that she couldn't take care of it herself, and Steven agreed and thought that was great. But if Mom and Dad saw her shoveling her own snow, they'd lose their minds.

If Dr. Taylor caught Steven working on her snow, she'd rush out and start shoveling too, trying to prove she was faster, stronger and in better shape than he was. It was bad enough to be beaten by someone so doggone old, but it was even worse because Dr. T. liked to talk a lot of smack while they raced.

"Hmmm," he said, using his mittened hand to stroke his chin, "if I do Dr. T.'s yard first, I'll be fresh as a daisy and will probably be able to finally beat—"

A loud, long, piercing whistle interrupted his train of thought.

Dr. T. was on to him. She had set her alarm for 4:30, just in case another one of these crazy snowstorms hit.

She'd looked out of her window and seen Steven standing on his porch stroking his chin.

She'd quickly thrown on a light jacket and cap and scarf

and done fifteen warm-up squats and twenty limbering lunges, then grabbed her shovel.

Dr. T. whistled again, then hollered, "Look at what just crawled out of his crib and decided to show himself! I hear the Kearsley Dam is flowing very nicely now, maybe you'd like to take another jump, flyboy."

Steven was very sensitive about remarks involving dams, since he and his dog, Zoopy, had fallen over a 250-foot one last summer.

Steven pouted. "Man! Isn't anyone going to ever let me forget that?"

Dr. Taylor said, "Oh, is snookums going to cry, or are you going to come off that porch? Because if you do, I need to warn you, I'm passing out booty whippings and mouthwash . . . and I'm clean out of mouthwash!"

Steven felt himself get very warm.

Who did she think she was?

He whipped off his heavy coat. It would only slow him down, and he was going to show Dr. T. that just because she was a university professor and close to a thousand years old didn't mean she could keep insulting him. No way was she anywhere near as strong as he was.

She stood at one end of the driveway, next to her garage, and Steven stood at the end nearest the street. The driveway was nearly a hundred feet long and the halfway point was a post where Dr. Taylor had put a sign, PARKING RESERVED FOR 1953 SKYLARKS ONLY! Which was the old car she drove.

Their eyes blazed across the snow, sizing each other up like a couple of gunslingers from the Old West.

Dr. Taylor finally gave a big fake yawn, twirled her shovel so fast it made a sound like a propeller, and said, "Anytime, whippersnapper, go for what you know."

Steven dug in, flipped a load of snow over his shoulder, *then* screamed, "Go!"

Dr. T. said, "Ha! You'll have to come up with a better way than *that* to cheat me, you juvenile delinquent!"

Snow began flying.

Steven had been *so* close to beating Dr. Taylor the last time they raced. It was only last week she'd beaten him out by pretending she was having some kind of attack. When he dropped his shovel and ran over to see what was wrong, she jumped up, finished shoveling and beat him by a second.

She was such a poor sport, she'd even taken the last shovelful of snow and thrown it in his face.

But today he wasn't falling for any sort of okeydoke.

Today he was going to stay focused.

Today he was going to keep the eye of the tiger!

Today the two-thousand-year-old professor was going down!

And Steven didn't care how spry or feisty she was!

He fell into a rhythm: bend, dig, lift, toss, bend, dig, lift, toss. The snow seemed to jump off his shovel.

It was important to concentrate, to try not to think about anything but the moving of snow. He especially knew that he couldn't think about the meeting of the Flint Future Detectives that was going to happen tomorrow morning, that that was the main thing he shouldn't be thinking about.

"Think about moving snow," he told himself.

Bend, dig, lift, toss, bend, dig, lift, toss.

"Keep the snow moving!

"Because," he thought, "if I start to worry about tomorrow's meeting, where I know that doggone Richelle Cyrus-Herndon is going to try to take over being president of *my* club, I'll lose my rhythm. If I try to figure out a way to stop Richelle, I might not keep moving snow as fast as I need to.

"Wait a minute!" Steven thought. "That's it! *Moving!* Maybe I can think of a way to trick Richelle and her parents into *moving* out of Flint! Or maybe if I come up with a *moving* sob story, she'll feel sorry for me and won't try to be president. Or maybe . . ."

Dr. Taylor started her trash-talking. She was shoveling a million miles an hour and talking at the same time.

He couldn't help himself, he looked up to see how far along she was.

It was unbelievable!

He'd taken a teeny head start, had stayed focused and worked so hard that sweat was pouring down his face, but she had shoveled just as much snow as he had!

"So, snookums," she yelled, "have you ever heard the song 'John Henry'?"

Steven told himself, "Ignore her, keep shoveling! Keep shoveling!"

"It's an old song about a strong, good-looking brother from back in the day who could lay down more railroad track than six other men at the same time."

Steven knew the song.

Dr. T. said, "So one day the boss brought in this steam drilling machine that could lay down as much track as *eight* men!"

Steven remembered that the machine and John Henry had raced to see who could lay a mile of track the fastest.

"John Henry smoked that machine just like I'm about to smoke you!"

"But," Steven thought, "didn't he *die* right afterward?"

"That's right, snookums, I'm 'bout to go John Henry on you!"

She began singing "John Henry" but changed the words of the song:

"Doc-tor Taylor . . ." Huwah!

"Told her neighbors . . ." Huwah!

"That their son ain't really all that bright . . ." Huwah!

"And when she is . . ." Huwah!

"Done whip-ping him . . ." Huwah!

"He will si-it . . ." Huwah!

"Crying in the night!"

"Oh, man, was that ever weak!" Steven thought. "If she thinks she can get at me with that sorry mess from the Stone Age, she's wrong, I'm gonna lay down some twenty-first-century, modern-day music on her, I'm gonna beat her down with some hot rap licks!"

Steven thought for a second and came back at Dr. Taylor:

"I listened to your song 'bout John H. and the
machine.
I can see you've been around and your mind is
still quite keen.
But please don't you forget, while John Henry
was the best,
When the race was done and over . . . they laid
his soul to rest!"

They were pacing themselves with the music. It was easy to keep a good strong rhythm when you had a beat like this. Dr. Taylor sang:

"Like John Henry . . ." Huwah!

"Whipped that steam drill . . ." Huwah!

"Is exactly what I am going to do . . ." Huwah!

" 'Cause a steam drill . . ." Huwah!

"And Steven C. . . ."

"Have exactly . . ."

"The-uh same IQ!"

The snow was flying, the music was flying and the insults were flying!

Steven couldn't help himself, he looked up again to see how close he was to the finish line. Another thirty-five shovelfuls to get to the pole, the same distance as Dr. Taylor!

He went into shoveling and rapping overdrive!

"I'm not at all surprised, Doctor,
You're 'bout as good as me.

14

Yo, word is out that you should be a pro.
'Cause looking at the history
Of the garden called Eden,
I see you were there and spent time shoveling
  snow!"

He could see he was going to do it!
Dr. Taylor was going to go down!
She had about nine more shovels to go and he had six!
"Yahoo!" Steven screamed to himself. "The kid has done
it again! Another one bites the dust!"
He pushed himself harder and tossed another rap at the
professor.

"Each day he's getting stronger . . .
Each day he shovels longer . . .
And today's the day that you
Ste-ven will conquer!"

He knew he shouldn't do it, but he couldn't help himself, he just had to check one more time.
His heart soared! He guessed she had four more shovels
to go. He had the one that he was throwing over his shoulder and one other, then he'd be the victor!
But something strange happened, and if you know anything about strangeness, you know it's a lot like bad news, it
always happens in threes.
First Steven looked up and saw that Dr. T. had disappeared!

"Okay," he told himself, "some kind of trick, some kind of trick! Don't stop working!"

He dug into the last shovelful of snow and the second strange thing happened.

He heard a very loud DONG! and thought, "Hmmm, I knew there'd be a lot of celebrating when I finally beat her, but I can't believe someone's actually ringing a great big bell."

The third strange thing happened:

The ground rushed up at Steven and his face crashed into a pile of the snow he'd just shoveled. The next thing he knew, he was napping soundly on Dr. T.'s driveway.

He started having the strangest dream.

The confused Canada goose landed and was nudging him with its beak! It looked like the goose was getting ready to burp, but instead it opened its mouth and a gusher of snow hit Steven in the face!

The goose waddled away, but when it did, it made a whirring mechanical sound.

"Hmmm," Steven thought, "a little too weird to try to understand right now."

He propped himself up on one elbow and tried to remember why on earth he'd taken a nap that early in the morning. The sun wasn't even up.

He looked down and noticed that his jacket had been put over him like a blanket.

"What? I don't remember doing that."

The snow under his head had been shaped like a pillow.

"Huh? I don't get it. Looks like I tried to make myself comfortable."

Then he remembered. The race with Dr. T.!

He stood up. Her driveway, porch and sidewalk had all been cleared. He looked over at his own yard and saw that all the snow was shoveled there too. Right to the edges! The same with the Millers' yard.

"Now, this *is* strange! I must've shoveled the Millers' yard, but I don't feel like I've been stuffed full of cookies, hot chocolate and old stories."

He scratched at his head and felt a big lump that he'd never had before.

"*Very* strange. I guess I did all that shoveling before I started snoozing. Ha-ha! You the man, Steven Carter!"

Then he saw the note pinned to his jacket.

He took it off and read:

Dear Dam-Diving Dodo,
    Ten minutes! All three yards! Beat that, you nincompoop! Youth can never overcome experience!
P.S. Mr. Miller is quite a delightful baker, isn't he?
P.P.S. Your parents will be receiving a bill for the big dent your head put in my shovel.

Steven rubbed his chin and said, "Hmmm, this looks like a case for the Flint Future Detectives! Maybe I'll do some investigating, look around, collect some evidence and figure out what happened here."

He noticed the sun hadn't risen yet and said, "Naah, I'll do it late . . ."

Oops!

" 'Oh, give me a home, where the buffalo roam!' "

He screamed out, "Yee-haw!" slapped the ground two times and hollered, "Braz-ohs!"

Rubbing the mysterious knot on the back of his head, Steven said, "The only thing I'm going to investigate now is how long it takes me to get back in bed and fall asleep!"

TWO

The Flying Spy Cam

ON THE TOP FLOOR of the downtown federal building Special Treasury Agent Fondoo's eyes were glued to the computer monitor in his office. He was studying an overhead view of the south side of Flint and a close-up of three houses covered in snow.

Fondoo called out, "Agent Malaney, get in here, the flying camera is working again!"

His new assistant opened the door and set her cup of coffee on Fondoo's desk. She couldn't believe she had to start work at four-thirty every morning, but that's how early Fondoo was here. He was sitting in his chair holding something that looked like a controller for a video game.

"Watch," Fondoo gleefully said as he wiggled the joystick, "the professor and that evil little troublemaker are having another race! My money's on the prof again! You're

19

gonna love seeing how crushed that Carter kid is when she beats him!"

Agent Malaney couldn't believe how much joy her boss was getting out of watching a tiny senior citizen and a little boy shoveling snow.

"It's great! You'll actually see his shoulders sag and his confidence disappear when she finishes before he does! And if I can get this camera to zoom in, we might even see a tear or two!"

Agent Malaney's eyes may have been on the screen, but her mind was wandering back to her last assignment in Florida. She wondered what had gone so wrong that she was now spending a winter in, of all places, Flint-freezin'-Michigan.

The official story was that she was Agent Fondoo's new assistant; the truth was that she'd really been sent to keep an eye on him. Madam Director, who was both the head of the Treasury Department and their boss in Washington, was very worried about his behavior.

Malaney and Fondoo both gasped.

The little boy was shoveling fast and furious, and as he strained at the snow, the professor calmly circled behind him, revved up her shovel a couple of times, then smacked him in the back of his head!

The microphone on the flying spy camera picked up a loud DONG!

Malaney yelled, "Why, that's assault and battery!"

Fondoo said, "Yes! And isn't it delightful? With a swing

like that I think she needs to be tested for steroids!" He laughed until tears began forming in his eyes.

Agent Malaney said, "Shouldn't we get out there and arrest her?"

Fondoo looked shocked. "Are you kidding? If we're really lucky, she'll whack him a couple more times. She's quite spry and feisty, you know."

Agent Malaney had been hearing for years about the strange things that went on in Flint, but she had absolutely no idea how really strange it got some of the time.

Fondoo pointed at the monitor, leapt from his chair and screamed, "No! What on earth is she doing?"

On the screen the professor walked over to Steven's porch and picked up the coat he'd thrown off. Then she made a pillow out of a pile of snow and gently put his head on top of it, gave him a kiss on the forehead and tucked his coat around him like it was a blanket.

"No! He's down! Hit him again! Finish him off!"

But it looked like the only things the woman was going to finish off with the shovel were her neighbors' yards.

Malaney watched the woman shoveling the snow and thought, "My goodness, she reminds me of that song where John Henry lays down railroad ties!"

Fondoo was crushed. He grabbed his coat and went to the door.

"I'm going to Halo Burger for a couple of chicken burgs deluxe, heavy mayonnaise and olives. If you need me, good luck, my cell phone will be turned off."

The door shut behind him and Agent Malaney quickly picked up the controller he'd dropped.

"I can't believe Fondoo would leave that youngster out there like that! I've got to check to see if he's okay."

She landed the flying spy cam and had it waddle over to Steven. It took her a second to learn how to control the camera, but she finally zoomed in close to the snoring future detective. She even had the camera's beak nudge him a couple of times to see if he was all right.

He seemed to be fine, just soundly asleep.

She tried to make the camera walk backward but hit a wrong button, and a gusher of snow poured out of the flying spy cam's beak.

"Oops!"

She gave the controller a good look and noticed the button on the back that read "Come Home."

She pressed the button, and the camera began to run, then took off into the air.

Two and a half minutes later it landed on Agent Fondoo's windowsill.

She shook her head. "What kind of sick mind would develop a camera and snowmaking machine that is shaped like a Canada goose?"

She knew, though.

She'd been briefed as to what had happened here in Flint with the quadrillion-dollar bill. All the Treasury agents knew how one mysterious Othello Chickee had given the little Carter boy a most unusual piece of money.

This had caused a panic in the Treasury Department because the bill was top-secret and very valuable. Madam Director posted a reward for the bill's return, and Fondoo found out this kid had it. He ordered a bunch of agents to get it back, and they ended up chasing the boy and a giant dog, Zoopy, until they fell over the Kearsley Dam. The Treasury Department never got the bill back, though, and Fondoo was in a lot of hot water for losing it and for endangering the boy's and dog's lives.

Everyone knew how badly Agent Fondoo wanted to get even with the little boy for getting him in so much trouble, and Malaney was supposed to protect the kid. But that wasn't the only reason she'd been sent to Flint. While she was going to have to give Madam Director a report on Fondoo, she was also supposed to try to find out if the Flint Future Detectives were still investigating what they called "Mr. Chickee's funny money." They'd solved only a part of the mystery, and if they discovered the rest of the secret, Madam Director had said, "heads and reprimands will roll."

Agent Malaney opened the window and the goose/spy camera hopped onto Fondoo's desk.

She thought it was wrong how Agent Fondoo was so hung up on this Carter kid and getting revenge, but she had to admit Fondoo's invention of this camera was brilliant.

It looked and flew and waddled and acted exactly like a large Canada goose, except that its eyes were the lenses of a camera. And except that when it was cold, it made a mechanical whirring sound as it walked.

Fondoo had also miniaturized a snowmaking machine and put it in the body of the goose. When Malaney first came to Flint, he had told her that the goose had been spying on a juvenile delinquent gang that called itself the Flint Future Detectives, and that they still hadn't caught on that the goose was fake.

But when winter came and it would snow, he couldn't have the goose leaving footprints near the Carter house, so he'd just have the goose shoot a couple of feet of snow in the area to hide the tracks.

That was the original plan, but once Fondoo found out that the Carter father made his son shovel all the snow, Fondoo started burying the kid's house even if the goose hadn't left any tracks.

Agent Malaney picked up the goose and put it in the closet where Fondoo kept it during the day.

She took out her notebook and wrote, "Strange things happening in Flint. I'm not really sure if Flint Future Detectives is a dangerous gang or just a club. Just because someone gives a bunch of kids a name or a label doesn't mean that's what they are. I don't think Fondoo can be trusted."

Man, if she only knew how true that last part she'd written was!

THREE

The Earth Trembles:
The Battle for the Presidency of the
Flint Future Detectives!

"**B**ANG!"

The next morning Steven pounded a sawed-in-half table leg on the top of his desk.

He looked around at the two other people and the giant dog in his bedroom and said, "I call this meeting of the Flint Future Detectives to order. Mr. Secretary, please take attendance."

Russell Woods stood up and cleared his throat. Taking attendance was his favorite job in the club. He looked at the piece of paper in his hand and said, "Is the honorable president, CEO, founder and number one detective of the club here today?"

Steven stood. "Present, Mr. Secretary." He sat back down.

Russell said, "Thank you," and drew a picture of a small box with a bow on it next to Steven's name.

He and Steven had talked about this quite a few times, but Steven hadn't been able to change Russell's mind. Russell was a really big kid for his age, but since he was only seven years old, Steven let a lot of things slide with him. To Russ it made a lot more sense to draw and color a picture of a present next to the person's name rather than to write "Present" or put a check mark there. Steven said the meetings would go a lot quicker if Russell did the drawing and coloring later, but Russell didn't seem to have too many other duties as secretary, so he really worked hard at the ones he did have.

He noticed that something was bothering Steven today. Most times when Russell was coloring the present Steven would sigh or shake his head, but today he didn't seem to mind as Russ fumbled through the box of colored pencils to find the perfect one.

Russell said, "Is the honorable dog handler, friend of the founder, secretary, number two detective and club bodyguard here today?"

He put the paper down and walked over to Steven's window. He turned around, looked back to where he'd just been standing and said, "All five of us are present, Mr. Secretary."

Russell walked back to the desk, picked up his list and, answering for each one of his five jobs, said, "Thank you. Thank you. Thank you. Thank you. Thank you."

This was one thing that Steven *had* been able to change Russell's mind about. Since Russell was the honorable dog handler, friend of the founder, secretary, number two detective and club bodyguard, he felt that each and every one of these jobs was very important and should get a chance to answer by itself. So he used to walk to five different places in the room and say "Present" five different times. Then he'd draw and color five different pictures of a present next to his name.

Steven told Russell he was going to have to cut him down to only one job because all the meetings were taking too doggone long. When Russell had to choose between fewer jobs and more coloring, the jobs won.

Russell started coloring the one box next to his name and shot a quick glance at Steven. It was usually around this time that Steven would turn into a bundle of twitches and nerves, but he didn't seem to care how long Russell was taking.

Finally Russell stood up again and said, "Is the chief protecting animal, the heart and soul of the FFD, the big kahuna and official getaway animal here?"

Russell put the paper down, stood up and walked over to the foot of Steven's bed. Zoopy, the gigantic dog that Russell's family had given to Steven, had flopped himself there and was right in the middle of one of his blue bunny dreams. Russell knew it was a blue bunny dream and not one of the pesky purple squirrel ones because there wasn't near enough drool coming out of the giant dog's mouth. For some reason nothing got Zoopy gushing like chasing one of those purple squirrels.

Russell grabbed Zoopy's upper and lower jaws, then made his voice go real deep. While moving the dog's mouth open and closed, Russell said, "Present, Mr. Secretary. Ah-oof! Ah-oof! Ah-oof! Ah-oof!" which was one bark for each of Zoopy's four jobs.

Russell's hands were soaked with Zoopy's slob, so he wiped them on his pants, walked back to the desk and started drawing the presents next to Zoopy's name. He sneaked another peek at Steven.

Again nothing.

Usually Steven would be close to losing his mind by this time.

Russell was starting to worry. Steven's ears weren't even wiggling; most Saturdays by this time his ears flapped so much that at least one piece of paper was blown off the desk onto the floor.

"Man," Russell thought, "I bet I could make Zoopy read one of those thousand-page Hairy Plodder books out loud and Bucko's ears wouldn't even budge. Something *really* is bothering him. Everything isn't irie at all, mon."

Russell said, "All present, Mr. President."

Steven said, "What? Huh? Oh! Fine, Mr. Secretary."

Richelle Cyrus-Herndon couldn't believe how disorganized this meeting of the Flint Future Detectives was, but after a look at the condition of Steven's room she thought to herself, "On second thought, it's no surprise at all."

Steven was so busy pretending he was ignoring Richelle that he hadn't noticed that Russell *was* becoming a better detective. Something *was* bothering Steven.

Steven had spent the last forty-eight hours . . . well . . . maybe it was the last forty-eight minutes . . . okay, okay . . . the last forty-eight *seconds* before the meeting trying to figure out what to do next. He'd been so desperate he'd even gone and pulled Great-great-grampa Carter's cranky old dictionary off the shelf and asked it for advice.

He'd given his best sigh before he said to the book, "So, it's like this, Richelle Cyrus-Herndon is going to want to join the Flint Future Detectives Club, and you know she's the smartest kid at Clark Elementary, so I kinda figure she's gonna want to be president. But everyone knows being smartest doesn't mean you automatically get to be president, so it doesn't seem fair that she should be able to come in here and just take over my job without at least—"

The cover of the dictionary flew open and Steven read on the copyright page, "*Whine, whine, whine.* Is there a point or question to all of this idle chatter, or is this merely a demonstration to show me what a pip-squeak ([PIP-skweek] *n. A contemptibly small or unimportant person, a twerp*) you have grown up to be, because believe me, you can stop, that point was made *long* ago."

"Man!" Steven thought. "There's still no love in Dictionary Land."

The letters on the copyright page rearranged themselves to say, "If it's love you're looking for, might I suggest checking out the phone book under 'Therapists' or tuning in to *Oprah.* If it's truth you seek, you've come to the right place."

"Okay, then," Steven said, "what should I do? I know as

29

I ask for new business at the meeting today, Russell
; to introduce Richelle and then the battle for the
ncy is going to begin. . . ."

The dictionary wrote, "Battle? Well, young Mr. Carter,
if what you're referring to as a 'battle' is based on merit
([MER-it] n. *Something that deserves or justifies a reward*) or
justice ([JUS-tis] n. *The quality of being just, righteous, fair*),
then I think your calling this a 'battle' may be an example
of extreme hyperbole ([high-PUR-buh-lee] n. *Rhetoric, obvious and intentional exaggeration*)."

The dictionary wasn't through. It wrote out, "I feel the
best description of the contest of Steven Daemon Carter
versus Richelle Cyrus-Herndon is a rather simple four-letter
word: rout ([rout] n. *A horrible defeat marked by disorderly
flight*). Let me demonstrate."

Steven sighed; he had the feeling this demonstration
wasn't going to make him feel a whole lot better.

The dictionary spelled out, "This is just like what will
happen at today's meeting."

The letters on the page bunched together in two groups,
the vowels on one side and the consonants on the other.
Over the vowels the word *Steven* appeared, and over the
consonants the word *Richelle* was written. Above their
names the words *Is there any new business?* showed up, and
without warning the vowels and the consonants charged at
each other and sparks flew, and sounds of metal slashing at
stone and smoke and confusion began to rise from the page.

The dictionary closed itself and the fight kept going on.

The old book jerked and bumped and burped and jumped until it seemed like it was going to fly off the table. For a second everything was quiet, then without warning a long string of frightened-looking, bruised and battered *e*'s squeezed from between the pages and, sounding just the way you'd think a long string of frightened, bruised and battered *e*'s would sound, they jumped off the edge of the table and fell to the ground in a cloud of smoke.

They screamed, "E-e-e-e-e!" then hit the floor with a loud BOOM!

Next came a string of torn and tattered, bruised and battered *i*'s, then *o*'s, then *u*'s, then *a*'s.

"I-i-i-i-i!" BOOM!

"O-o-o-o-o!" BOOM!

"U-u-u-u-u!" BOOM!

"A-a-a-a-a!" BOOM!

The cover on the dictionary came open, and the consonants had a group of *y*'s shaking and quaking on the edge of the page. The consonants were arguing amongst themselves whether or not they should make the *y*'s jump. They were debating if the *y*'s were *really* vowels or consonants.

Steven could feel his spirits sinking.

"But wait a minute," he said, "you're just a dictionary, and as far as I can tell, you're a dictionary with a chip on its shoulder, and from reading Mom's book *Things with Chips on Their Shoulders*, I know that's a sign of not feeling good about yourself. So why would I listen to what you have to say?"

The cover of the dictionary came open and Steven slammed it shut without reading what was written there.

"I know it's going to be something smart-mouthed and negative, so I don't need to read it. If I'm going to beat Richelle Cyrus-Herndon for the presidency of the Flint Future Detectives Club, I'm going to have to go in with a positive outlook, I'm going to have to be strong!"

Steven straightened his shoulders and stood tall.

"Besides, if it really is going to be a rout, why are the y's still hanging on so tough? As long as the y's are fighting back, I've got a chance! If I'm going to stay as president of the club that I put together, then I have to be ready to fight and think and be quick on my feet! I'm going to have to float like a butterfly and sting like a bee!"

Steven began dancing around the room, ducking and bobbing his head.

"If I'm going to keep what's mine, I'm going to have to do what I did to Dr. T., I'll have to go in with the eye of the tiger!"

Steven started ducking and bobbing and growling and looking mean while he danced around the room.

He threw his hands above his head and screamed, "Yes! Yes! I'm ready! Cyrus-Herndon is through! This is my club, this is my house, this is my world, baby, Richelle's just a squirrel trying to get a nut!"

Steven's dad had peeked in the room to see what the big ruckus was, saw his son ducking, bobbing, weaving, growling and looking mean, and thought to himself, "Some of the time I don't know about that boy."

Now Steven said to Russ, "Is there any old business that needs to be taken care of?"

Russell looked at his paper and said, "No, Mr. President, all that business is what we secretaries call moldy-oldie and isn't worth talking about anymore."

Steven was geeked! Steven was ready! He took a deep breath, swallowed hard, said to himself, "Eye of the tiger, eye of the tiger, eye of the tiger . . . ," then asked, "Okay, is there any *new* business that we need to take care of?"

Russell said, "Yes, Mr. President, I've thought up a new way for us to make a bunch of money to put in our savings account."

This wasn't what Steven was expecting.

"Really?"

"Really. Remember when the big power blackout came last year?"

"Uh-huh."

"Remember how all the phones stopped working and all the ovens and stoves and microwaves stopped cooking?"

"Yeah."

"And remember how my mummy wanted to call for a pizza to be delivered, but there weren't any phones that worked?"

"I wasn't at your house, but I believe you."

"And remember how hungry I was and—"

Steven said, "Mr. Secretary, what is your moneymaking plan? We don't have all day."

"Well, I figured out a perfect way to solve that problem and get lots of cash!"

"What, Russell, what?"

"What's the stupidest bird you know about?"

"Mourning doves." Steven almost asked what in the world that had to do with power failures and making money, but he knew once Russell started telling one of his schemes, the best thing to do was to go along for the ride.

"Okay, and a mourning dove looks a lot like a pigeon, right?"

"I guess so."

"And pigeons get trained to deliver messages, they can fly for hundreds of miles, can't they?"

"Yes, Russell."

"Okay, here's my plan, and it solves all the problems when the power goes out and you're hungry."

Steven waited.

"All we got to do is train *chickens* to deliver messages! They're a little smarter than pigeons, and when there aren't any phones and you're starving, all you have to do is get a message delivered to you by a chicken. Then you read the message a-n-d . . ."

Russell dragged the word out waiting for Steven to answer.

Steven gave a confused look to Richelle, who was looking just as confused.

Finally Steven said, "You read the message and what, Russell?"

Russell said, "And you eat the chicken!"

Richelle Cyrus-Herndon couldn't bite her tongue any

longer. She felt that there were times you had to let some of the ridiculous stories people told just slide, but when something was extremely ridiculous, you had to set the person straight.

She said, "But how would someone know to send you a mess—"

Steven banged the table leg on his desk.

"You're out of order! No one called your name to speak. You're gonna have to be quiet. You're not even a Flint Future Detective yet!"

Richelle shook her head, tapped her foot and chewed her lip.

Steven needed the meeting to move on. He needed to get to the new business that would require all of his training and strength.

"Wow, Russell!" he said. "That's a great idea, we'll work on that one later. Now, is there any other new business?"

Russ cleared his throat. "Yes, Mr. President, we have two new people who wanna join the Flint Future Detectives Club."

Russell reached in his front shirt pocket and opened his hand. There in the middle of his palm sat the world's shiveringest, shakingest, quiveringest, quakingest little dog, Rodney Rodent.

Steven couldn't believe his eyes. It looked like Rodney Rodent was even smaller than he'd been a couple of days before!

Russell said, "The first person is Rodney Rodent, and I

think he'd be a good club member because he's great at not getting noticed, he doesn't eat anything but cheeseburg deluxes with heavy olives, and even Daddy says he's the best because he hasn't barked or done anything annoying yet. The only sound he makes are funny little whines."

Steven said, "And what job should Rodney Rodent have in the club, Mr. Secretary?"

"Well, Mr. President, since he's so good at getting in places without anyone seeing him, I think he would be perfect as the Flint Future Detectives number one sneak. He can also be the official map reader and number one bug chaser."

Steven said, "If anyone objects to Rodney Rodent becoming the number one sneak, official map reader and number one bug chaser, let them speak now or forever rest in peace."

The room was quiet. But Richelle's eyes rolled so hard they did almost make a sound.

"Oh, man," Steven thought, "here we go! Eye of the tiger, grrrrr! Eye of the tiger, grrrrr! Eye of the . . . ," then he said to Russ, "Is there any *other* new business?"

"Yes, Mr. President, one other person would like to become a member. . . ."

Richelle Cyrus-Herndon said, "Excuse me. I said I'd *think* about being a member, and after I've seen how this meeting is run, I'm not so sure I'd . . ."

Steven had a flash of honesty with himself; he knew

that the smartest person really *should* be in charge. He knew Richelle really was probably better qualified to be president. He knew she'd probably find better things to investigate than he had. He knew he should let her be the leader.

He knew all of that, but he still couldn't bring himself to show Richelle any respect.

He said, "Oh, yeah? Really, huh? You think I'm going to fight you over this? Well, I'm not! Go ahead! You can be president! It's not the great job you think it is!"

Russell said, "If anyone objects to Richelle Cyrus-Herndon becoming the new president of the Flint Future Detectives, let them speak now or forever rest in peace."

No one spoke. No one said a peep. In fact, the only sound that could be heard came from the room where Great-great-grampa Carter's dictionary was kept, and that sound went something like this:

"Y-y-y-y-y!" BOOM!

And if Steven had bothered to look at what the dictionary had written to him, he would have seen:

"Capitulation ([kuh-pit-you-LAY-shun] *n. The act of complete and total surrender. Giving up when confronted, with no realistic hope of winning. In other words, 'You got played big-time, Bucko!')*"

When Steven finally did check the dictionary a couple of days later as part of his new job as the Flint Future Detectives chief looker-upper, he read, "The word is out that you are no longer president of the club. Alas, so this is how it ends, not with a bang but with a whimper. What a wuss ([woos] *n. A weakling, a wimp*).

And even though Steven would be doggoned if he was going to look up *whimper*, he didn't know why, but all of a sudden he let out a long, moaning cry mixed with low, plaintive broken sounds.

FOUR

The Evil Mural!

ALMOST A WEEK LATER Russell Braithewaite Woods was in the middle of another weird dream.

In this one Richelle Cyrus-Herndon said, "Oh, Russell, I can't be president of the Flint Future Detectives anymore. I need you to take over, because we all know who's *really* the smartest kid at Clark Elementary! And who is also the handsomest and the best eater of lots of food!"

Then in the dream Steven said, "Oh, yes, Russell, not only are you a large and powerful eater of all kinds of food, you are also the best friend Zoopy ever had. Please, please be president of the club and please, please take Zoopy back home with you. Does anyone object to Russell being president or will you all forever rest in peace?"

Zoopy said, "I second that emotion," and made a sloppy,

slurping sound, which is what you do if you've got a mouth that's always full of gallons of drool and slob.

That wasn't the weird part of the dream, that was the good part. The weird part began when Rodney Rodent said:

> "I haven't worked in so, so long I think I've lost
> my mind,
> I can't believe I came to Flint an Old Soul for to
> find.
> I've moved their stove, I've moved their fridge, I
> carried them real far.
> If I can get to the garage, I'll even move their
> car."

After making those bad rhymes, Rodney Rodent picked up the bed, with Russell on it, and walked around the room carrying it over his head while saying:

> "Russell is the greatest! Russell is the king!
> Russell is a chomping, chewing, fast-eating
> machine!"

But like with so many great things, this dream came to an end way too soon.

Russell was instantly awake when he heard his mother scream.

A second later he heard her say, "The fridge? The stove? How could they steal the stove and fridge without anyone hearing them?"

Russ was pretty sure he was awake, but what he saw when he looked around his room made him think maybe his weird dream was still going on.

First because his bed had moved from one side of the room to the other, and second because where his bed used to be now sat a refrigerator and stove!

Russell blinked a couple of times and shook his head to try to make the kitchen appliances go away, but each time he opened his eyes, they were still right there, right where they weren't supposed to be.

"Wow!" Russell looked at Rodney Rodent and said to the dog, "I bet I won't need a crystal ball to tell that some big trouble's right around the corner."

Russell's mummy walked into his room. "Russell, did you hear anything last night? Someone stole the . . ."

His mummy froze with her mouth wide open.

"Boy!" Russell thought. "Maybe I should ask Mummy to join the Flint Future Detectives—she noticed the stove and refrigerator were in my room, and no one gave her *any* kind of clues!"

She didn't say another word, just turned around and walked out of the room like nothing unusual had happened.

Five seconds later she was back with Daddy. She pointed at the fridge. "Impossible, huh? I'm mad, am I, huh? HUH?"

Daddy looked at the stove and fridge, then at his son, then at his wife, then back at their appliances.

Mummy said, "That Carter boy is involved in this. I don't know how, but I feel it in my bones that that Steven Carter boy has something to do with this."

Daddy said, "Russ-ell, muh boy, ya didn't hear no one toting the icebox into ya room last night? Ya slept right t'rough it? And I s'pose it'd be a grand waste of time ta ask why ya drag ya bed from one par-factly good side of the room to the otha, huh?"

Russell had seen Steven stroke his chin whenever he wanted someone to think he was doing some real strong thinking, so he decided to do the same.

"Hmmm," he said, "I did dream that Rodney Rodent picked up the bed and was marching me around the room. I didn't see him touch the stove and fridge, but he might've. The way he was carrying my bed around the room, I kinda think he's a lot stronger than he looks."

Mummy said, "Was that Carter boy over here last night?"

"No, Mummy, Steven's real brave, but he's afraid of you guys."

"Imagine that! That little monster afraid of *us*!"

Daddy said, "I'll hafta go rent a dolly to move these t'ings back. What a city, what a country!"

Mummy shook her head and left the room.

"All right, muh boy, our mornin's all set for us. Get dressed and let's get goin'."

After Russell had washed his face and brushed and flossed his teeth (yup, he actually flosses!) and combed his hair, he dropped Rodney Rodent into the front pocket of his shirt and went into the kitchen.

Since he was a soon-to-be-great future detective, he

42

noticed something was missing, and not just the stove and refrigerator either. Every other morning there was the delicious smell of breakfast being cooked when he came into the kitchen. Today there was nothing.

"Oh, man!" Russell thought. "This would be a great time for a messenger chicken!"

His father was sitting sadly at the kitchen table.

"Daddy, what are we gonna do about breakfast?"

"We can't do no cookin' till the fridge and stove are outta ya room, muh boy. It's too-too late for breakfast anyway, and ya mutha is craving cheeseburg deluxes with heavy olives from Halo Burger, ya up ta riding shotgun?"

As soon as Daddy said "cheeseburg deluxes with heavy olives," Rodney Rodent began twitching around in Russell's shirt pocket. The strange little dog wouldn't eat any of the dog food the Woods family bought him, but he sure had developed a real taste for olive burgers.

Russell said, "No thanks, Daddy, I don't want to go there unless you can borrow our old van from the Carters and I can borrow Zoopy from Steven."

"Why is it ya won't go ta Halo Burger without that wretched animal? Ya t'ink I haven't taken note of that?"

"It's not Halo Burger that I don't want to go to, it's that terrible parking lot that you leave the car in when you go inside."

"Ah! Why I hafta marry a Flint gal? Muh own dear mutha tole me I shoulda never leave Jamaica! Children there would never talk sich nonsense."

"Yes, Daddy, and children in Jamaica never have to sit and wait in any parking lots as scary as that one either."

Russell's daddy was feeling a little stressed by the wandering kitchen appliances and the fact that he'd missed breakfast. He was in no mood to hear any nonsense about scary parking lots from his son.

"That's it, boy! In the car. Now! And this time you're showing me what's so terrible about this insane parking lot. If ya doe learn ta overcome ya fears, they'll sure overcome ya!"

Russell thought, "It's good I have Rod-Rode in my pocket—at least there'll be one dog there to protect me."

Russell really did have some pretty good reasons not to want to go to Halo Burger without protection. One big reason was it was in that parking lot that he'd been attacked and robbed by a pack of hungry dogs not so very long ago.

An even bigger reason was the horrible, frightening Vernor's ginger ale mural that was painted on the wall there. Steven's father had told them it was put up in 1932, during a time in America's history known as the Great Depression.

After Great-great-grampa Carter's dictionary told them that *depression* meant "low spirits, gloominess, dejection and sadness," Russell had to agree, whoever had drawn this mural had to be the saddest, most gloomy person in the world!

The mural was painted on the whole side of a four-story-tall, one-block-long building and showed a world that made adults smile and say things like "What a great imagination that artist had!" or "Isn't that cute, I wonder how the artist thought that up?"

But kids? Kids knew!

They knew in their hearts, in their bones, that there was nothing to smile about in the painting. They understood that whoever had painted this mural had been to the strange world it so clearly showed and had had a very, very, *very* rough time there! Young people *knew* this world was real! Real and horrible.

Where old people saw a cute, cartoonish advertisement, young people saw a deadly serious warning.

The left-hand side of the mural showed a castle wall with a window about five feet up. Nothing so bad there, but what was in the window was responsible for Russell, Steven and a whole bunch of other young Flintstones having spent many a night with their eyes wide open and sleep the last thing on their minds.

It was a gnome.

And that's the perfect word to describe it. Through the years some people had said it was an elf or a sprite or a leprechaun or a goblin or even a troll, but kids knew that none of those words came *anywhere* close to painting a true picture of what it was.

It was a gnome. Pure and simple, a gnome.

To describe something as scary and weird and unreal looking as this thing, you needed a word that was just as scary and weird and unreal looking.

Gnome was it.

Gnome it was.

Great-great-grampa Carter's cranky old dictionary might define *gnome* as "one of a species of diminutive beings, usually described as shriveled, little old white men, that inhabit the interior of the earth and act as guardians of its treasures." But Russell was closer to the truth when he defined *gnome* as "that thing in the parking lot of Halo Burger that would chew through your ribs, then gnaw your heart out of your chest if you gave it the chance!"

There were seven or eight other gnomes working away on moving barrels full of ginger ale, and some of them were even smiling pleasantly, but the one in the window was obviously the boss, and he obviously got to be boss because he was the meanest.

This gnome had an unusually large head and was wearing an old conquistador-type helmet. Nothing too horribly scary there. The scary thing was that the gnome was peeking out of the window with a pipe in his mouth and smiling the weirdest smile that had ever been seen on Earth. People may talk about how mysterious the *Mona Lisa's* smile is, but it's obvious that anyone who does has never seen *this* grotesque, gnarly, gruesome, gnomic grin!

To make matters worse, the gnome was winking!

At what, no one knew, but he had winked at generations of Flint's residents. Many, many winters, springs, summers and falls he had looked out on downtown Flint with this weird smile and this scary wink.

And if that isn't enough to make someone not want to

go sit in a parking lot while his mom or dad runs in for a burger, I don't know what is.

As they drove toward the restaurant, Russell's daddy popped in a Bob Marley CD.

Russell started moving to the beat of the reggae music. He probably would've started grooving anyway, but he knew if he didn't, his father would threaten to put him out of the car. According to Daddy, "If ya can't get in the groove, there's no point in ya riding wit' me!"

Russell felt his heart beating faster with each block as they drew closer to the restaurant. Even though he was in Russell's shirt pocket, Rodney Rodent seemed to be getting more and more anxious and excited too.

"Man," Russell thought, "my heart's beating so loud and fast that it's messing with Rodney Rodent's sleep! This can't be good."

But it wasn't Russell's heart that was getting Rodney Rodent worked up, and it wasn't the thought of cheeseburg deluxes with olives either, it was something else. The tiny animal was sensing something that he hadn't sensed in the longest, and it was what he'd been looking for ever since he came to Flint and started living with the Woods family. He could tell that he was very close to the doorway to his other home!

When Daddy turned left off of Saginaw Street into the parking lot next to Halo Burger, Rodney Rodent jumped right out of Russell's pocket onto the dashboard and began bobbing his head up and down.

Daddy thought he was either imitating one of those little fake bobble-head dogs that some people had in their cars, or that his son's dog had decided to keep time with the thumping reggae bass!

Mr. Woods was shocked. "My word! I doe t'ink I've evah seen that little t'ing move so much, what on eart' is wrong wit' it?"

Russell said, "See! I told you there was something spooky about this parking lot! Can't we park somewhere else?"

And then, almost as if to make Russell's point, Rodney Rodent stopped bobbing and stared at the mural Daddy had parked in front of. For the first time since he'd moved in with the Woods family five months ago, he threw his head back and howled! And it was like he'd been saving five months of howls in his itsy-bitsy body. It was so loud that it seemed like he must've been saving five *years* of howls!

The howl was so strong that the window next to Russell's father shattered and blew out into the parking lot! Three car alarms went off. The man who was waiting on people at the drive-through window threw his headphones down and, just like Russell and his father, slapped his hands over his ears to try to block this terrible screech.

Then, as suddenly as he'd started, Rodney Rodent stopped.

The car wobbled a little from side to side. Russell saw his father's lips moving, but the only thing he could hear was an echo from the incredible shriek.

"Mercy me!" Daddy's words finally got through to Russell. "I t'ought that was the par-fact animal! That t'ing is bad as that terrible hippopotamus dog we give to ya daft little friend, that Carter boy! I 'ope I'm not going ta be spending as much money on windows with this one as I spent on food for that otha monsta!"

Russell's father opened the car door, got out and peeked back in through where his window used to be. "Ya stay here. If anyone come a-asking what the noise was, tell 'em ya doe know! I gotta get ya mutha the olive burgers. What a city!"

Rodney Rodent hadn't moved from the dashboard; he was acting as if the mural had hypnotized him.

"Rod-Rode! Don't look at that thing! I have a bad feeling about those gnomes!"

But Rodney Rodent wasn't about to pull his eyes off of the mural. And if Russell had looked carefully, he would've seen there was one spot in particular that the tiny animal's eyes were locked on. He was staring at the pipe-smoking gnome who was peeking out of the window and winking, the one Russell and every other young Flintstone hated looking at the most!

Russell reached toward the dog to put him back in his pocket, but before his hand could wrap around him, Rodney Rodent jumped out of the window and flew right at the mural!

"Rod-Rode!"

The tiny dog shot directly at the mural going about 120 miles an hour! Russ knew if Rodney hit the wall going with that much speed, he'd break his neck and be flattened like a slow squirrel on Dort Highway. It didn't seem as if there was anything that could stop him!

Russell hoped he was still asleep and this was some weird slow-motion dream.

"Wow!" Russell thought. "I haven't seen anything this strange since the night after I set the record for cheese and onion enchiladas at Los Aztecos!"

He noticed how Rodney's ears were pressed against the sides of his head as he sped at the wall. He noticed how the dog's tail was spinning like a propeller, making him go incredibly fast. He noticed how, when his friend was just a few inches away from certain death, Rodney Rodent closed his eyes and opened his mouth again and said the first thing he'd said since they'd picked him up at the dog pound. Instead of the little whining sounds he'd always made before, the dog said in English, as clear as anything, "Bow-wow-wow-yippee-yo-yippee-yay!"

All of this was very strange, even for downtown Flint, but what happened next made Russell think he'd gone from being in a dream to being in a nightmare! The winking gnome, the one that looked the meanest, came to life! He stopped winking and both of his eyes and his mouth flew open in surprise!

Just as Rodney was about to smash into the wall where the gnome was painted, the creature ducked and Rodney sailed over his head and right into the painted-on-the-wall window! When the tip of the dog's tail disappeared into the blackness behind the gnome, a sound like something very large and heavy crashing into water came from the wall.

The gnome popped back up, looked behind himself, turned around and stared hard into Russell's eyes. After what seemed like two hours the gnome showed a row of tiny, filthy pointed teeth, winked again and went right back to being a painting!

When Daddy came back with a bag full of cheeseburg deluxes heavy on the olives, he found his son outside the car standing next to the Vernor's mural. Russell was on his tiptoes, reaching up and sticking his finger out toward one of the gnomes, then quickly jerking it back, sort of like he expected the painting to take a nip out of him.

Daddy thought his son was mumbling something like "Rot wrote, rot wrote, rot wrote, rot wrote . . ." over and over.

"Oh, no!" Russell's father shouted. "The wee dog's scream has scrambled the boy's brains! I doe t'ink his mutha's gonna take this one too good!"

Daddy opened the back door of the car, and just like he used to do for the six months that Russell had been small enough to fit in a car kiddie seat, he put his son in, buckled the seat belt and patted Russ on the head.

"Doe ya worry, boy, everyt'ing's gonn be irie, just ya wait and see."

Daddy pulled the car onto Saginaw Street and turned his reggae back up. Russell started bouncing with the groove in the backseat.

Daddy looked in the rearview mirror and said, "Oh-ho! What I tell ya? There ain't not'ing that a little bit of Bob Marley and the Wailers and the smell of cheeseburg deluxes heavy on the olives can't cure real good and quick! How ya feeling, boy?"

Russell knew he had to ease his father's mind or there'd be a ton of questions. And maybe even counselors.

He said, "I'm fine, Daddy, all I was doing out there was overcoming my fears before they overcomed me."

"Now, that's muh boy! Spoken like a true Jamaican, mon! Everyt'ing irie?"

"Everything's irie, Daddy."

"And the little elf t'ing ya was poking in the nose ain't giving ya no messages or not'ing, is he?"

"No, Daddy."

"Good, good. How 'bout the rest of 'em? None of the otha elf t'ings is telling ya ta set no fires nor bite no one, are they?"

"No, Daddy."

"And ya got that little dog quieted down in ya pocket? We won't be having no more busted-out windows, will we?"

Russell patted his empty shirt pocket and said, "Rodney Rodent's going to be so quiet it will seem like he's not even here."

"Wonderful, boy. And we agree ya mutha doe have no need ta know 'bout what happened wit' the little dog and the car window? She gets winda this, she might want ta get that giant Zoopy back from those crazy Carters."

"We agree, Daddy."

"Sweet and dandy, son, sweet and dandy!"

Russell knew better than to say anything to his mother *or* his father about what had happened. Some things are so odd that telling an adult about them doesn't do anything but get you a bunch of worried looks, whispered conversations and visits with school counselors. That was a lesson he'd learned when he tried to explain to his teacher about Zoopy and the pesky purple squirrels. Russell figured there were some things that you really shouldn't tell anyone who was responsible.

"But who can I tell about this?" Russell thought. "Who won't blab and get me in trouble?"

Nothing came to him.

He stroked his chin a couple of times, the way you do when you're trying to make people think you're doing some real serious thinking.

Almost magically a name and a face came to him!

"Man!" Russell thought. "That chin-rubbing stuff really works! I'll tell the most irresponsible person I know, I'll tell Bucko!"

And Russell was right, anyone who'd ride a huge dog over a 250-foot dam *must* be extremely irresponsible. Why, they must be the *king* of the Irresponsibles!

FIVE

Dad Saves the Day! (By Sheer Luck!)

RICHELLE CYRUS-HERNDON was very excited. Saturday, the day after Rodney Rodent disappeared, was the first meeting of the Flint Future Detectives that she'd be in charge of. And she couldn't wait to show these knuckleheads the proper way to run a meeting.

She pounded the sawed-in-half leg of a table on Steven's desk and thought, "Hmmm, one of the first things I'm going to do is to get a real gavel."

She said, "I hereby call this meeting of the Flint Future Detectives to order. Mr. Secretary, would you please take attendance?"

Russell cleared his throat and said, "Is the new president, the smartest kid at Clark Elementary School, the one who understands big words and the first new human joiner of the Flint Future Detectives here?"

Richelle said, "I'm present, Russell, and I think from now on, to help speed things up, you can just call me by my name."

"Uh-oh," Russell thought, "another president who wants to run things her way. I'm gonna have to break this one in too."

He cleared his throat. "Is the new vice president, second-smartest kid at Clark Elementary School, chief looker-upper and founder of the Flint Future Detectives here?"

Steven weakly raised his hand.

Russell called all five of his jobs and all four of Zoopy's.

Richelle started twisting her mouth from side to side and tapping her foot.

Then Russ said, "Is the official sneak, map reader and bug chaser here?"

He knew the answer to that one, but he was hoping that Rodney Rodent might show up for the meeting anyway.

No answer.

Russell said, "Four club members present, one missing, Madam President."

Richelle said, "Thank you, Mr. Secretary. Is there any old business?"

Steven said, "Yes, the old business is to find out why the chief bug chaser isn't here today."

Richelle said, "Yeah, where is Rodney Rodent?"

Russell looked up from his present-coloring and said, "The last time I saw him he was splashing into the window with that mean gnome on the Vernor's mural."

Steven said, "Ooh, I know the one you mean. That thing looks like it's haunted, I hate that painting."

"Not as much as me, and now it's ate up Rod-Rode and I don't know how to get him back."

Richelle said, "Russell, you've got to explain better than that. How did a painting eat up Rodney Rodent?"

Russell told what had happened at Halo Burger the day before.

Richelle said, "And the gnome showed you his teeth, then winked at you and froze again?"

"Yup."

Steven said, "Russell, the last time you said something that weird was right after you set the record for eating the most falafel in half an hour at the Shawarma Shack. You haven't been back there, have you?"

"No, Bucko, this really happened."

Richelle squinched her left eye halfway shut and left her right eye halfway open. She twisted her lips to the left and then to the right. She tapped her foot around a million times before she said, "You know what, Russell? I believe you. I think this is something we need to investigate."

Richelle went online with Steven's new computer. She searched for "Vernor's mural Flint" and soon had a picture of the mural on the screen. She read the sign that was painted in the bottom right-hand side of the painting.

ORIGINALLY PAINTED IN 1932

Steven said, "If that sign was telling the truth, it would say, 'Terrifying Flint's young people since 1932.' "

Richelle said, "Whatever. So Russell, you said Rodney Rodent actually talked and said something before he disappeared into the wall?"

"He sure did, it sounded like cowboy talk."

Steven stroked his chin and said, "Hmmm, cowboy talk. Did he say 'Yee-haw'?"

"Uh-uh."

"Did he say 'Keep them dogies movin' '?"

"Nope."

"Did he say 'Whoopee-tie-yi-yo'?"

Richelle said, "Would you *please* stop asking him these idiotic questions? You're out of order. What exactly did he say, Russell?"

"Well, Richie-Rich, I'm not sure if I got it exactly right, but now that I think about it a little more, it was something like cowboy talk and doggy talk all mixed together."

Steven said, "Did he say 'Woof, woof, reach for the sky, Tex'?"

"Uh-uh."

"Did he say 'Arf, arf, howdy, ma'am'?"

"Nope."

"Did he say—"

Richelle banged the table leg and screamed, "Order! Order! Would you be quiet for a minute so he can tell us what Rodney Rodent said?"

Steven looked hard at Richelle and finished, ". . . 'Bow-wow, saddle 'em up, pardner'?"

Richelle growled.

Russell said, "That's it! That's half of it, anyway. I remember half of what he said was 'Bow-wow!' The rest sounded like a cowboy song."

Steven said, "Did it sound like 'Home on the Range'?"

"Not really."

"Did it sound like 'The Streets of Laredo'?"

"I don't think so."

Richelle said, "Did it sound like 'If Steven Carter Doesn't Close His Big Mouth, I Think I'll Die, You-all'?"

Russell said, "Not that one either."

She said, "Do you remember anything at all about the way it sounded, Russell? It may be a key to how Rodney Rodent disappeared into that mural."

Russell looked very disappointed in himself. He kind of mumbled, "Sorry, Madam President, I guess I wasn't paying real close attention."

Richelle said, "That's easy to understand, Russ, seeing your dog disappear into a mural behind a winking elf has got to be pretty scary. I can understand why you might be a little traumatized."

Steven said, "Yeah, Russ. Besides, we're Flint Future Detectives, it's an easy enough mystery for us to solve."

Richelle said, "Since I'm president, I want to try some new things with the club and this is a good place to start. Instead of chasing off after every little thing like you guys used to do, I think it would be best if we concentrated on only one thing with each meeting. As president, I move that we end this meeting now and head over to the Vernor's mural to find out exactly what happened to Rodney Rodent. It's our duty to try to rescue him and bring him home. I also move that we keep this top-secret until we get more information. Does anyone second my motions?"

Russell said, "If it means getting Rod-Rode back, then I don't mind getting a little dramatized by that terrible painting. I second that emotion."

Just as Russell said that, Steven's father walked by the door.

" 'I Second That Emotion'! Great song! Smokey Robinson and the Miracles. Actually, it was the first song they got into the pop top ten after they changed their name. They used to be known as just the Miracles. It was released June 13, 1967, written by Smokey and Al Cleveland. Got to number one on the R & B charts and number four on the pop charts. What are you guys talking about, Motown?"

Steven thought, "Oh, no! Dad's going to start going off about African American musical history again. I've got to stop him!"

He said, "No, Dad, we're trying to find out what happened to Rodney Rodent. He disappeared down by Halo Burger yesterday."

Dad walked into the room. "Disappeared?"

Russell said, "Hello, Mr. Carter. Yup, he disappeared in thin air right behind that winking gnome."

A shiver ran through Steven's father. "Ooh, that thing has given me the creeps ever since I was a kid, I don't know why they don't just paint over it."

Russell said, "Yeah, it was even creepier when Rod-Rode started talking before he disappeared in the mural."

Mr. Carter lost interest. He said, "Isn't that nice? Well, I'm sure if you wait long enough, he'll come back. Hello, Richelle."

"Hello, Mr. Carter."

He looked at Zoopy, who was drooling a little lake onto the floor of Steven's bedroom.

He said, "Here's an idea! Why don't you take Zoopy down there and see if he can disappear into the mural too, you know, to give Rodney Rodent a little company."

Steven said, "That's not funny, Dad. We're trying to fig-ure out what Rodney Rodent said before he flew into that window. Maybe if we knew, we could go in behind him."

If Mr. Carter had lost interest before, it was nothing compared with the way he wanted to get out of the room now!

"Uh-huh, talking dogs, mystery songs and ducking elves. I'm sure this is something you guys will solve in no time at all." He started easing toward the door.

Russell said, "Yeah, it was cowboy talk and doggy talk all jumbled up together."

Mr. Carter patted Russell on the head and said, "I'm sure it was, son, I'm sure it was."

He looked at his watch and said, "Is it really that time

already? I'll bet there's something I'm supposed to be doing, and if not, I'll bet I'm going to pretend there is. You three keep having fun. Never stop dreaming!"

Dad closed the door and thought, "I wonder if Russell has been setting any more food-eating records? What an imagination!"

Richelle gave Steven and Russell a very disappointed look. "So much for us keeping this secret. You two have got the biggest—"

The bedroom door came open. Mr. Carter said, "Cowboy talk and dog talk all blended together?"

"Yes, Mr. Carter. But I can't remember what it was."

"Hmmm," Steven's dad said, "cowboy talk and dog talk all jumbled together. Why is that ringing a bell?"

Dad snapped his fingers and said, "I know! That sounds a lot like the lyrics from one of our underappreciated musical geniuses from the mid-sixties, George Clinton."

Steven groaned.

"In perhaps his most famous song, 'Atomic Dog,' released May 10, 1970, he used the unlikely combination of cowboy vernacular and doggish sounds to produce a classic."

Russell said, "What's a vernacular?"

Steven didn't know, but he sure wasn't trying to look anything up in Great-great-grampa Carter's cranky old dictionary. He said, "I'll explain it to you later, Russell. Well, Dad, we were just getting ready to do some research on . . ."

But Dad wasn't through. Steven thought that was one of

the problems with old people, once they got started rolling down a road on something, they didn't stop till they were at the end.

"Vernacular is the everyday language of a particular group of people, Russell. In this case it means cowboy language. Let's see, maybe I can sing a bit of it for you."

Steven was horrified! Who wanted to come and listen to someone's father sing musty old songs from the Stone Age?

Dad cleared his throat and sang, "A-tom-ic daw-uh-awg, bow-wow-wow-yippee-yo-yippee-yay, bow-wow-yippee-yo-yippee-yay . . ."

Russell screamed, "That's it! That's what Rod-Rode said before he disappeared into the mural!"

Richelle said, "I hereby call this meeting of the Flint Future Detectives over! All members are to put on your coats and boots, go home and get permission to meet at Halo Burger in ten minutes. Or if you can't get permission, you have to figure out a way to sneak out and meet us there in fifteen minutes."

Dad said, "Hey, wait a minute, I heard what you said!"

Richelle said, "We know, Mr. Carter, but you're so cool we know you won't rat us out on this important mission."

Steven looked at Richelle like she was nuts. His father? Cool? Not even Dad would buy that nonsense.

Dad smiled ridiculously and said, "Why, thank you, Richelle, how perceptive of you to know I used to be known as Daddy Cool when I was a bit younger! I guess that's something that fades a bit but never goes completely away, huh? And you're right, I'm not going to rat you out. Just don't be long and be very careful."

Dad left the room.

Russell said, "If we're gonna look in that window with that elf, we need to take a stepladder or something to stand on, it's pretty high up."

Steven said, "We can use what I use to reach things on the high shelf in the book room, Great-great-grampa Carter's dictionary."

Richelle said, "All right, gentlemen, Halo Burger, fifteen minutes."

SIX

If Richelle Cyrus-Herndon Jumped off a Five-Story Building, I Suppose You'd Follow Her Then Too? or Welcome, *Whose* Highness?

By THE TIME RICHELLE got to the sidewalk on Saginaw Street, Steven and Russell were already waiting. Russell's head was shooting from side to side like he was expecting to be attacked at any minute. Steven was squeezing a large book to his chest, trying hard not to look too scared but failing miserably.

"Good," Richelle said, "I thought you guys might've started without me."

Russell looked at Steven and Steven looked at Russell.

Russell said, "Are you kidding, Madam President? I was waiting for you. I'm not going anywhere near that mural again unless there's a real responsible person with me. Sorry, Bucko."

Steven couldn't say a word. When you've ridden a giant

dog off a 250-foot-tall dam, you get a lot of remarks like this. And you can't really argue with them. You're just about what Great-great-grampa Carter's dictionary would call "defenseless."

Richelle said to Steven, "And what about you, why are you just standing here, did you already check the mural out?"

"I . . . uh . . . I didn't want to leave Russ all by himself."

Richelle snatched the dictionary away from Steven and marched toward the mural. "I can't believe you two great big guys are afraid of a silly painting. I thought Flint people were supposed to be so hard and . . . whoa!"

Richelle stared up at the gnome.

She whistled and said, "Wow, I can see how that thing *could* scare somebody!"

She set the dictionary on the ground under the painting and stood on it to get a closer look.

Russell took a step back and turned his face away. "Be careful, Madam President, he's gonna show you his teeth, and it looks like him and Mr. Toothbrush haven't talked in a long, long time."

But the painting didn't move.

Richelle reached toward the wall. She jabbed at the gnome and finally touched it and traced his head, even rubbing at his pipe and beard.

"Russell, are you sure Rodney Rodent disappeared here? Couldn't it have been a really bad dream? This just feels like a regular wall with some scary paint on it to me."

Russell said, "No joke, Madam President, Rod-Rode sang that song Mr. Carter sang and, presto-change-o, he was gone."

Richelle said, "What was the song again, Steven?"

Steven said, "Bow-wow-wow-yippee-yo-yippee-yay."

Richelle said, "I don't know . . . ," and before she could get another word out of her mouth, a thick-fingered pair of greenish orange hands popped out of the mural and grabbed each of her shoulders.

The boys' mouths flew open as the gnome snatched Richelle off the dictionary and into the window. The last thing they saw before Richelle disappeared in the blackness behind the creature was the bottoms of her shoes. Then they were gone, and the boys heard something large and heavy crashing into a pool of water!

The gnome slowly looked from Russell to Steven. As soon as he saw Steven, he smiled, showed a row of razor-sharp, not-very-clean-looking teeth and bowed twice before he closed his mouth. Then, winking again, he turned back into a flat painting.

The boys were in such a state of shock that instead of running off screaming like anybody with half a brain would have done, they stood there looking at each other with their mouths wide open.

Russell finally said, "Hey, Bucko, did you see the fingernails on that thing? They were yellow and long and pointy, and it looked like he hadn't cleaned underneath 'em in a hundred years."

Steven shook his head a couple of times and said, "What just happened, Russell? Wasn't Richelle here a second ago?"

Russell said, "Uh-oh, Bucko, I think you must have got dramatized too. That gnome grabbed her."

Steven said, "That's what I thought. Well, she's a pain in the neck, a know-it-all, a blabbermouth and a pest, but she *is* the president of the Flint Future Detectives, so you know what that means we have to do."

Russell said, "Yeah, run out of here like we've got half a brain. I was just about to get started!"

Before he could turn around, Steven grabbed his wrist. "Uh-uh, Russ, we're Flint Future Detectives, we've got to protect each other no matter what."

"I know, Bucko, but I was thinking I could do a lot more protecting if I was at home."

"Russell, you know we've got to go in there after her to make sure she's all right."

"Man, Bucko, I never thought I'd say the same thing my mother said, but if Richelle Cyrus-Herndon jumped off a five-story building, I suppose you'd follow her then too?"

Steven wrestled Russell over to the wall under the painted-on window. Using all the strength he had, he pulled his friend up on the dictionary and sang, "Bow-wow-wow-yippee-yo-yippee-yay!"

From where they were they saw the gnome's eyes come to life; they were so close they could even feel warm, swampish-smelling air coming out of his nose. They looked up into his nostrils and saw a couple hundred hairs with tiny bits of nose candy dangling off some of them.

Not only didn't this gnome take very good care of his fingernails or his teeth, sitting in a drafty window for so many years had given him a pretty bad cold too!

The creature's dirty hands reached out and snatched Steven by his collar. Russell squirmed out of Steven's grip and had just about rolled away when the gnome's fingers clamped around his ankle. Russell grabbed at anything he could but only managed to pick up Great-great-grampa Carter's cranky old dictionary.

Then, as if the boys and the dictionary were as light as three grains of rice, the gnome tossed them over his shoulder into the blackness of the little window!

The gnome growled, "Welcome, Your Highness!"

Before they disappeared, Russell yelled, "I hope he's the scariest thing in here, 'cause if he isn't, I'm really not going to be too hap—"

The sound of something very large and heavy crashing into water filled both of their ears. A blackness surrounded them that was so powerful and thick that it seemed to smother everything, even their thoughts.

Good thing too, 'cause both boys were having almost the same one and it wasn't the sort of thought you'd think a couple of future detectives would have, especially not two from Flint.

Steven was thinking, "I want my mommy!"

Russell was thinking, "I want my mummy!"

As the darkness began to lift, a whining, winding-down sound, like a giant vacuum cleaner had just been switched off, came through first; then their sight and their thoughts returned too.

Steven looked at Russell and Russell looked at Steven.

They were sitting on the front steps of a wide porch.

Russell shook his head, rubbed his eyes and said, "Man, Bucko, am I ever glad to see you! I'm having the worst nightmare! That terrible monster at Halo Burger finally snatched me and pulled—"

"Russell, it isn't a nightmare, that gnome did get us, we came through the window behind him!"

Russell continued, ". . . and then in the nightmare you told me that it really happened! I can't wait till I wake up and tell you about this for real!"

"Russell, this *really* is happening."

A voice from behind them said, "It took you two long enough to get here."

Steven's eyes rolled.

Russell said, "Richie-Rich! You aren't going to believe this crazy nightmare I'm having, in it Bucko keeps telling me it's real and you're standing over there tapping your foot with your arms crossed and your lips twisted up the same way you do when I'm awake!"

She said, "Russell, I think you've been traumatized again. This isn't a dream or a nightmare, this really is happening. And where did you get that thumb drive? I never noticed that before."

Richelle pointed at the silvery computer thumb drive that was hanging around Russell's neck.

Russell raised it so that he could get a better look.

The thumb drive said, "Oh! This is a nice change of pace, not only have I lost ninety-nine point nine seven percent of my weight, but if you'll excuse me for a moment, I'm currently downloading information that is increasing my data storage by an amazing seven thousand and fifty-nine percent!"

Steven instantly recognized the voice. Even though he'd never heard it before, he knew this was Great-great-grampa Carter's bad-dispositioned dictionary!

He frowned and said, "Oh, great. Not only is it light enough to carry around, it can actually talk."

The dictionary said, "Don't hate, celebrate! And please be quiet while I momentarily shut down to gain all of this new knowledge."

Russell laughed and handed the thumb drive to Steven. "Wow! Here, Bucko, this is yours. This is the weirdest nightmare!"

Richelle said, "Russell, you've got to get hold of yourself, this is not a nightmare."

Russell said, "Nice try, Madam President! If this was really happening, would Mr. Chickee be sitting under that tree with a newspaper in his lap talking to that tall, skinny African lady? I don't think so. Take my word for it, I've had nightmares like this before."

Steven and Richelle looked where Russell was pointing,

and sure enough, the man who was sitting in a tall leather chair with his back turned toward them did look a lot like Steven's friend who was blind, Mr. Chickee. But this man *was* reading a newspaper.

The boys jumped off the porch and ran toward the man and a tall, thin woman in African dress.

The man threw his head back and laughed. There were no ifs, ands or buts, this was Mr. Chickee!

SEVEN

The Return of Mr. Chickee

"M̲R̲. C̲H̲I̲C̲K̲E̲E̲?"

The man turned his head, and as soon as the boys saw his face they froze.

"Oops!" Russell said.

"We thought you . . . ," Steven started to say. "Wow! Are you Mr. Chickee's twin brother?"

The man looked from one boy to the other. "Steven! Russell! How are my two favorite Flintstones?"

Russell whispered, "Not a nightmare, huh, Bucko? I think we're having a dream about clones, this guy looks exactly like Mr. Chickee except he isn't carrying a cane and I think he can see."

The man laughed. "Steven, close your mouth. What would Mr. Mitchell at the corner store say if he saw a Flint

Future Detective looking so . . . well . . . so goofy? He'd probably stop you from ever buying Vernor's and Paramount potato chips."

Steven was shocked! Every Saturday morning he and Mr. Chickee used to go to Mitchell's Food Fair and get pop and potato chips. Who else but Mr. Chickee would know that?

"You *are* Mr. Chickee!"

Mr. Chickee smiled and opened his arms to give the boys a hug, but they seemed stuck, like their feet were set in concrete.

Mr. Chickee turned to Richelle and put out his hand. "Othello Chickee's the name, it's a pleasure to finally meet you. Welcome to Ourside."

Richelle shook the offered hand.

"My name's Richelle Cyrus-Herndon. It's nice to meet you, sir. I've heard a lot about you, but I was starting to wonder if you were nothing but Steven's and Russell's minds playing tricks on them."

Mr. Chickee laughed and said, "They do have two of the wildest imaginations I've ever seen, which is one of the reasons I'm so fond of them. Another reason is you'll never make two other friends who are more loyal and true."

Richelle wrinkled her brow and said, "Humph!"

Steven and Russell were still staring at each other in a state of shock.

Steven looked at Russell, then back at Mr. Chickee again, then back at Russell, then back . . .

Russell looked at Steven, then back at Mr. Chickee, then back at Steven again, then back . . .

It was hard to believe there was even one drop of common sense between the two of them!

Richelle shook her head. "They're the only two people I know who can get brain freeze without even drinking a slushie! As you can see, they don't handle surprises and new ideas very well."

Mr. Chickee smiled and said, "But as *you* know, there aren't two bigger hearts in all of Yourside."

Richelle snuffled again. "That's the second time you've said something like that, Mr. Chickee. Where on earth are you talking about when you say 'our side' and 'your side'?"

"Yourside, one word, capitalized. And that's exactly right. It's right on Earth."

Richelle twisted her lips to the right, wrinkled her brow and tapped her foot.

Mr. Chickee said, "Once the three of you came through the porch, you landed in Ourside, one word, capitalized. You left what we call Yourside, which is your Earth."

"So we're not on Earth anymore?"

"Technically, it's iffy. Earth is another dimension of here, or here is another dimension of Earth, no one's quite sure."

Richelle began tapping her left foot and said, "I hate sounding like Steven Carter, but huh? I don't get it."

"Don't get yourself all worked up, Ms. Cyrus-Herndon, it will become clear after you've been here for a while."

"A while?" Richelle started tapping her foot even faster. "If I'm not back home in fifteen minutes, my mother will be down here looking for me. She'll turn Yourside, Ourside and Theirside upside down. She'll—"

"Hold on, hold on. I need to explain that right away. You see, time is different here in Ourside."

Richelle's foot was tapping so fast that her shoelace came undone and retied itself four times.

"A countdown has started, Richelle," Mr. Chickee said, and handed her a really strange-looking watch. It didn't have hands or numbers or anything that would make you think it was telling time; instead it spelled out the words, "Twenty-nine days, twenty-three hours, fifty-six minutes, and thirty-two seconds," and it was counting down a second at a time.

Richelle turned hers over several times in her hand. "What is this?"

"That is an Oops-a-Daisy. It tells how much time you can spend here before one second passes on Earth."

Richelle looked at the watch thingy, calculated and said, "So that means we can be down here for thirty days, a whole month, and only one second will go by on Earth?"

"Correct."

"So then if we're down here for two months, only two seconds will go by on Earth?"

"No! Exactly wrong. That's why I'm giving you this. Once you're here for one second more than one month, once this Oops-a-Daisy counts down to all zeroes, I'm afraid ninety-nine years, nine months and nine days will have passed on Earth.

"I have to make certain you understand that, Ms. Cyrus-

Herndon. If you stay down here one second more than a month, more than ninety-nine years will have passed on Earth and nearly everybody you know will have died before you get back. The only person who'll probably still be alive is Steven's neighbor, Dr. Taylor. It will be as though you've been frozen and have come back almost a hundred years later."

Richelle reached the Oops-a-Daisy back toward Mr. Chickee.

"Thank you very much, but we won't be needing this. We're just looking for Russell's dog, Rodney Rodent. Once we get him, we're bye-bye."

Mr. Chickee's forehead wrinkled. "I'm hoping it isn't going to be that simple, Richelle."

It took that long for Steven's brain freeze to finally thaw out.

He said, "Huh? I don't get it. You can *see*, Mr. Chickee? You're not really blind? Andre, Smudge, Daniel and Stevie Boy Collins were right when they said you've been *pretending* you were blind all of this time? You've been tricking us? I can't believe it!"

"Steven, Steven, Steven. I've never pretended anything with you. When I'm on Earth, on Yourside, I truly am blind. When I'm here, in Ourside, I can see."

Steven said, "Huh? I don't—"

Mr. Chickee interrupted, "We're not exactly certain why, but intragalactic, translateral, cosmal, xenogenistic, fifth-dimensional continuum travel is not as easy to do as it sounds. Moving from Ourside to Yourside does have its problems. And while we're around ninety-nine point nine nine percent successful in keeping a person whole when they go through the porch, that last point zero one percent has presented us with some rather interesting and thus far insurmountable difficulties."

Richelle said, "That sounds like nothing at all, Mr. Chickee, one-hundredth of one percent sounds like a drop in the ocean."

"A very good analogy, Ms. Cyrus-Herndon, it is an extremely small amount, but at the same time it is *not* nothing. As small as it is, it does make a tremendous difference.

"Take my eyes as an example. Here in Ourside I have full use of them, I am completely sighted. But when I travel to Yourside, to your Earth, when I cross through the porch, something as small as a drop in the ocean changes, something that our greatest scientists have figured is less than point zero one percent of the total. That tiny bit doesn't work properly and I'm unable to use my eyes."

Richelle said, "But wait a minute, Mr. Chickee, does that mean the same thing happened to us when we crossed from Earth to here? Is there something that is point zero one percent different on us now?"

"Excellent question, Ms. Cyrus-Herndon, and the answer is yes."

Steven whispered to Russell, "Man! I was just about to ask that myself. She shoots her mouth off so quick no one else has a chance to—"

Richelle said, "But we all can see, we all can hear, what's different?"

"You never know. It affects each person differently. It might be something as minor as your hair is one shade lighter, it might be as trivial as your left earlobe is a millimeter longer or it might be something so major that it causes you to lose your vision."

"Hmmm," Richelle said, "I'll have to keep a watch on this."

"Yeah," Steven chimed in, "me too."

Richelle rolled her eyes. "Well, we see whatever has changed with you, Steven Carter, it's not your ability to think on your own, that's still as lame as ever."

Steven turned and looked at Richelle for the first time since they'd landed in Ourside. He knew he couldn't let her get away with saying that in front of all these people.

"Is that right, Cyrus-Herndon?" He looked right in her eyes. "On you I can see the point zero one percent change is . . ."

"Man," he thought, "I never noticed before that there's something kind of cute about Richelle when she's tapping her foot and rolling her eyes like that.

"Now, what was I about to say?" he asked himself. "Oh, yeah . . ."

"On you, Richelle, it's real easy to see . . ."

He thought, "It's real easy to see you're about the most beautiful person I've ever seen!"

A look of disgust swept over Richelle's face. "Why are you looking at me like that?"

"Like what, sw—" Steven quickly slapped his hand over his mouth before the last word he was going to say to Richelle came out. He couldn't believe it, but he'd been *that* close to saying "Like what, sweetheart?"

Russell said, "Yeah, Bucko, the way you're looking at Madam President is giving me the creeps!"

Richelle said, "If it's giving you the creeps, think what it's doing to me! I feel like I've got the heebie-jeebies, the walking willies and the creepy crawlies all at the same time."

Russell looked like a stomachache was coming on and said, "And what were you getting ready to call her, Bucko?"

Steven quickly looked away from Richelle and it seemed like his mind came back to him.

He said, "I was starting to say 'Like what, sw . . . sw . . . sweat hog! That's it! I was gonna say 'Like what, sweat hog?' "

Mr. Chickee and the African woman laughed.

The woman put her hand on Steven's head and said, "Hmmm, I think I see what has changed on *this* one."

Mr. Chickee sighed and said, "Ah, Naomi, do you remember?"

"How could I ever forget? I'll always remember my first love."

Steven slapped his hands over his eyes, Richelle slapped her hands over her mouth and Russell slapped his hands over his ears, and all three screamed, "Noooo!"

Sounding a lot like the Godfather of Soul, Steven kept

his eyes shut and pleaded to himself, "Please, please, please, don't let this be true. Please!"

He pulled his hands down and thought, "Okay, think like a detective, try to put things together. It seems like something has changed when I look at Richelle. When I think about her, I can't stand her, I know what a rotten, stuck-up little brainiac she is. I know she's about the worst person I've ever seen, I know she stole my presidency from me and I've got to pay her back.

"But when I see her face"—he opened his eyes, looked at Richelle and moaned to himself—"all I can think of is another one of Dad's weak old rhythm-and-blues songs: 'Heaven must be missing an angel, 'cause you're here with me right now!' "

Steven shut his eyes, shook his fist at the sky and screamed out, "No! Anything but this! I want something else to be changed! Make it so I'm not so smart, make it so I'm not so handsome, make it anything but this! What have I done to deserve this?"

He looked at Richelle, saw the horror on her face and screamed, "What have I done to deserve this, to deserve living at the same time as the most beautiful, most precious thing to ever have lived in history?"

Richelle's face went from being horrified to something Steven didn't recognize.

Great-great-grampa Carter's dictionary finally stopped downloading all of the new information and said, "Ah, that would be a classic look of mortification."

Steven's eyes were glued on Richelle. He said, "So, *mortification* means 'lovely beyond belief'?"

The African woman said, "Not quite. But simply avoid looking at her, young man, I'm fairly certain that will solve your problem."

Steven looked away, and sure enough, as soon as he did, he was back to thinking of Richelle as a creepy little genius wannabe.

He knew he had to say something extremely rude, but all he could come up with was "Richelle Cyrus-Herndon is such a pain that no one can stand her." He knew that was weak, so he threw in "She also eats boogers!"

Richelle smiled and said, "Whew!"

Russell smiled and said, "Whew!"

Steven, being careful to look at anything but Richelle, smiled and said, "Whew!"

Mr. Chickee said, "Well, now that that's over, I've been remiss in not introducing you to my dear friend Ms. Naomi Tiptip. Ms. Tiptip, this is Russell Braithewaite Woods."

Russell shook the tall woman's hand and said, "I recognize you! Mummy and Daddy force me to read all the time, and they bought me a book about people in Africa. I know you're dressed like a Masai woman. The book says your people do a lot of cattle herding."

Ms. Tiptip smiled and said, "You're right! I think it's great your parents encourage you to read and to learn about other people."

81

"Yeah, the book says the Masai are very friendly and never get angry at anybody."

Ms. Tiptip and Mr. Chickee exchanged a look.

She said, "Indeed we are a friendly people, Russell, but I'm not really sure what the book meant when it said we never get angry. Believe me, I've seen my sister get quite angry with my brother, and I must admit I've been known to get a little ticked off with him myself."

"Are you sure you're Masai?"

"Without doubt."

"I don't know, the book said real plain that you guys are the kind of people who have no mads in the group."

Ms. Tiptip smiled. "Ahh! Nomads! That doesn't mean we never get angry, Russell, it means we're wanderers, we travel from place to place."

Russell whispered to Steven, "I'm gonna ignore her definition, I like mine better."

Ms. Tiptip said, "Guess what, Russell? I've also studied a few things about you. I know you hold many Yourside records for eating massive amounts of food. In fact, I believe the only person in Ourside, in our dimension, who can consume as much as you do is the Incredible Bottomless Pit Glutton Man of Sultana."

Mr. Chickee said, "I don't know, Naomi. Don't forget, on the island of Cyclopsia there's Bryanne the Wonky One-Eyed Goat Girl, and she's even less picky about what she'll eat than the Glutton Man."

Russell beamed and whispered to Steven, "Wow, Bucko!

82

I never thought I'd be famous in another dimension! I don't even know what a dimension is!"

Mr. Chickee said, "And this charming young woman is Richelle Cyrus-Herndon."

Richelle said, *"Jambo, bibi. Habari gani?"*

The African woman laughed, threw her head back and said, *"Swahili! Jambo! Ulijulia wapi kuongea Kiswahili sanifu hivyo?"*

Richelle said, *"Niliishi Kenya miaka mitatu."*

Ms. Tiptip said, *"Nimefurahi sana kukutana na mschana kama wewe anayeongea lugha yangu vizuri sana!"*

Richelle said, *"Asante sana! Sijafanya mazoezi juzi juzi."*

Ms. Tiptip said, *"Unaongea vizuri sana. Naamini tutapata nafasi nyingine ya kuongea."*

Richelle said, *"Natumai hivyo pia. Nimefurahi sana kukutana nawe!"*

Ms. Tiptip said, *"Nafikiri ni vizuri tuendelee kuongea Kiigereza tena. Naamini kwamba marafiki zako wanafikiri tunawasengenya!"*

Richelle smiled and said, *"Ni kweli, wao si vijana werevu hivyo. . . ."*

Russell looked at Steven and Steven looked at Russell.

Steven said, "What a show-off. So what? Richelle Cyrus-Herndon speaks a little Spanish. Big deal. So does everyone in Puerto Rico."

He looked at Richelle, his eyes lit up and he said, "And my, my, my, what a beautiful Spanish accent that precious little cupcake has!"

He snatched his eyes away and said, "E-mail to self: No more looking at Richelle. Look other way no matter what. Can't forget this one."

Richelle pointed a finger at Steven and said, "If you say one more crazy thing to me, I'll hit you so hard you'll think Thor's popped you with his hammer."

Mr. Chickee said, "And finally, Ms. Tiptip, this confused-looking and -acting young man is my dearest friend from Yourside, this is Steven Daemon Carter."

"A pleasure meeting you, Steven."

"Pleeztameetchew, Ms. Tiptip."

Russell said, "Mr. Chickee, is it okay if I ask you a question? I was looking at that newspaper you were reading and something got me real confused."

"What is it, Russell?"

Russ pointed at a headline that read: STRANGE YOURSIDE WEATHER: RIO DE JANEIRO SNOWSTORM, SIXTY BRAZILIANS MISSING!

Mr. Chickee said, "Ah, that is a bit confusing, we're not sure why it's snowing there."

Russell said, "That's not what's got me confused, what I don't understand is how many is a brazilian?"

Mr. Chickee looked at Ms. Tiptip.

Ms. Tiptip looked at Mr. Chickee.

Richelle's eyes rolled.

Steven saved the day by saying, "I'll explain it to you later, Russell."

Richelle said, "Mr. Chickee, when I told you we weren't

going to stay here long, you said you hoped it wasn't going to be all that easy for us to get back to Flint. What did you mean by that?"

"Richelle, I'd suggest we go to my home to work this out, there's someone there who can explain everything."

Russell said, "Yeah, Mr. Chickee, I'm starting to get kind of hungry, do you have something to eat?"

Mr. Chickee said, "Of course I do, Russ. I know you're really going to enjoy it too. So what do you say, Flint Future Detectives? Shall we go? It's a very short walk to my porch."

A WORD FROM GREAT-GREAT-GRAMPA CARTER'S DICTIONARY
You are very fortunate that I can also translate Swahili. Here is what Ms. Tiptip and Richelle Cyrus-Herndon said to each other:

Richelle said, "Hello, madam. How are you?"

The African woman laughed, threw her head back and said, "Swahili! Hello! Where did you learn to speak such perfect Swahili?"

Richelle said, "I lived in Kenya for three years."

Ms. Tiptip said, "It is such a pleasure to meet a young woman who speaks one of my languages so well!"

Richelle said, "Thank you very much! I haven't had much practice lately."

Ms. Tiptip said, "You're doing beautifully. I'm sure we'll have plenty of time to speak later."

Richelle said, "I hope so. It's really good meeting you!"

Ms. Tiptip said, "I think we'd better start speaking English again. I'm sure your friends think we're talking about them!"

Richelle smiled and said, "You're right, they're not the smartest couple of boys you'll ever meet. . . ."

And in any language that you care to choose, Richelle Cyrus-Herndon sure is right about that!

EIGHT

Huh? I *Really* Don't Get It!

Mr. Chickee opened the door to his home and said, "Welcome!"

Steven, being the great detective that he was, noticed something odd and said, "Mr. Chickee, this looks exactly like your place in Flint!"

"Yes, Steven, that was done deliberately. In the beginning it made it much easier on me when I went to Yourside if I was already familiar with everything."

Steven said, "The only difference is that the table where you used to keep your sound system is empty."

"Not really, we have a different type of technology here. I don't mean to be curt, Steven, I hope we'll have plenty of time to discuss this later; now, however, we must get moving quickly."

Russell said, "Yeah, we really need to move fast, Mr. Chickee. All I want to do is find Rodney Rodent and get back to Flint in time for dinner. Have you and Ms. Tiptip seen a real shy, little, nervous-acting dog?"

Mr. Chickee and Ms. Tiptip looked at each other. She said, "Yes. Russell, the animal you call Rodney Rodent came through here yesterday, but he's gone back home."

Steven moaned, "You mean we let that gnome grab us for nothing? Rodney Rodent is safe? He's already back in Flint?"

"No. He is safe, but he's back at his other home, his home here in Ourside."

Mr. Chickee said, "Rodney Rodent was sent to Flint to lead you to us. You coming here was no accident."

He sighed. "This is kind of complicated and contains a lot of new information, so maybe you boys should have a seat before the brain freeze sets in again."

Steven said, "Boys? What about her?"

He looked at Richelle. "I'll sit if I can sit next to my darl—"

Richelle balled her hand into a fist and Steven quickly looked the other way.

He told himself, "No looking! No looking! Very important!"

He and Russell sat down on a couch in front of Mr. Chickee's empty round coffee table.

Mr. Chickee said, "Your adventure with the quadrillion-dollar bill was a test designed to see if you were capable of completing a series of missions that the Old Souls have set up for you. It was felt if you could pass that test, then you might be able to help us understand the prophecies of the Chronicles of Zornea-Hu. And Steven, I must say we were quite worried for a while, but you did enough things properly with the mystery of the quadrillion-dollar bill to pass."

Steven puffed his chest and started to look at Richelle to make sure she was hearing all of this, but Russell slapped the back of his head and said, "Please, don't look at her, Bucko, please don't shame yourself any more than you did already."

Mr. Chickee continued, "You didn't do great, but you did pass, just barely."

"Mr. Chickee!" Steven said. "We did better than barely pass, you can ask the feds in Washington. Madam Director knows the Flint Future Detectives solved the mystery of the quadrillion-dollar bill."

Ms. Tiptip said, "Actually you solved only a portion of it, but Mr. Chickee argued so strongly in your defense that the rest of the Old Souls gave you a pass."

"A pass? I didn't even know I was taking a test, and who are the Old Souls?"

"It's a group of people here in Ourside who have come together to try to save our world."

"Save it?"

"Yes," Mr. Chickee said, "save it. Sad to say, but what you see around you is a dying world."

He showed them his wrist. There was another one of the

Oops-a-Daisies there, but this one read thirty-two days, seventeen hours and forty-eight seconds.

Richelle said, "Are you saying that's all the time that Ourside has left before it dies?"

"That's it. If the mystery isn't solved by the time this Oops-a-Daisy zeroes out, the Chronicles of Zornea-Hu predict our destruction will be unstoppably set in motion."

Ms. Tiptip said, "Ah, Othello, they seem like such nice children, but those looks! Have you ever seen such expressions of confusion? Play the Holo-Vision for them, it's only fair that we flum-flub them to make sure they're completely informed. Especially since we are asking them to risk their lives."

None of the Flint Future Detectives said anything, but each one was thinking, *"Risk our lives?"*

Richelle looked at Russell, then at Steven.

Russell looked at Steven, then at Richelle.

Steven, who was slowly smartening up, looked at Russell, then at the floor in front of Richelle.

Mr. Chickee said, "Of course you're right, Naomi. Children, please make yourselves comfortable and watch the tableau there."

He pointed at the round coffee table where Steven and Russell were sitting. "I'll turn on the Holo-Vision and all of your questions will be answered."

Mr. Chickee clapped his hands twice and the lights in the room dimmed.

Russell said, "Mummy has a Clapper to turn off the lights too."

"Yes, Russell, it's brilliant, isn't it? It's on the list of the top ten things ever invented in Yourside."

Russell said, "Really? Is the magic U on the list too?"

Ms. Tiptip said, "The magic U? I'm not familiar with that. Dictionary?"

Great-great-grampa Carter's thumb drive dictionary said, "I'm drawing a big blank on the term, Ms. Tiptip. And considering the person who asked the question, I think perhaps this is something we might not want to pursue."

Ms. Tiptip said, "No, I'm not familiar with the term 'magic U' and would like to know what it means."

Russell said, "Yeah, Ms. Tiptip, it should be on the list of greatest inventions too, Mummy invented it. If you're not at home and you've gotta use the bathroom, you need to make a magic U."

Steven sighed. "Russell, maybe you can tell them about this later."

Ms. Tiptip said, "No, I'd like to hear about this if it doesn't take too long. What exactly is the magic U and what does it have to do with using the bathroom, Russell?"

"Mummy told me if you're not at home and have to use a strange toilet, you've got to be real careful 'cause they have a ton of germs and cooties on them. The only way to keep those things from jumping on you and making you sick is by taking three sheets of toilet paper and putting them on the seat in the shape of a upside-down U. For some reason the germs and cooties and junk can't get at you because the U is magic and stops everything from attacking you when you sit down."

Mr. Chickee and Ms. Tiptip both began blinking rapidly. It seemed the Flint Future Detectives weren't the only people who could look very, very confused very, very quickly.

Great-great-grampa Carter's thumb drive said, "I'd never stoop to saying 'I told you so,' so instead I'll quote one of my favorite Yourside situation comedies, 'Uh toad uh so!' "

After a few seconds Mr. Chickee said, "Perhaps we should just watch the Holo-Vision."

He clapped twice again and a man the exact height of a can of soup appeared in the middle of the table.

He bowed elegantly and said, "Welcome, one and all."

Russell and Steven were amazed!

Richelle, on the other hand, was not so impressed.

"Oh," she said, "I get it! *Holo-Vision* stands for 'holography vision.' "

Ms. Tiptip said, "Actually, my dear, it's quite a bit more complicated than mere holography, and what you're seeing is much more than a hologram."

Russell said, "A holo-what?"

Richelle said, "Isn't a holograph or hologram where a negative is produced by exposing a high-resolution photographic plate, without camera or lens, near a subject illuminated by monochromatic, coherent radiation, such as from a laser, and when it is placed in a beam of coherent light, a true three-dimensional image of the subject is formed?"

Mr. Chickee smiled.

Russell looked at Steven.

Steven looked at Russell and whispered, "Lucky guess."

Ms. Tiptip put her fist out and said, "Put it here, sister girl!"

Richelle gave Ms. Tiptip some dap.

Great-great-grampa Carter's cranky dictionary said, "Oh, boy, I have a strong feeling that that definition sailed positively miles over the heads of two of the people who heard it."

Steven said, "Ha! I get it! They explained about this on PBS. It only looks like that little guy is standing there on the table, but he really isn't. He's just a kind of moving picture, like a 3-D movie. He looks real, but he's nothing but light, you can even wave your hand right through him."

Steven reached over to do just that. Big mistake.

Ms. Tiptip said, "No! Don't tou—"

Too late.

The little man tried to duck but Steven was too quick. His hand smacked the man and sent him sailing off the table. He landed in a heap on the floor.

Mr. Chickee gently scooped him up, set him on the table and said, "Please forgive him, Horton, he's new here, they're from—"

The diminutive man said, "They're from *Yourside*! Who else would be so rude as to touch someone like that?"

Steven said, "Huh? I don't get it. I didn't know . . . I'm sorry."

Horton said, "Oh, you just *think* you're sorry. You wait. We have a saying here, 'Payback is a sandwich best served on stale bread.' And believe me, Mr. I-Can-Touch-

Anything-I-Want, either I or one of my Holo-Vision partners is going to pay you back *big* for this insult!"

He pointed at his wrist, where a tiny Oops-a-Daisy was strapped, and said, "And don't think just because time is getting short that you'll get away. We'll get you before this thing zeroes out, and that's a promise!"

Ms. Tiptip said, "Horton! Such hostility! I'm surprised! I know everyone here is under a lot of pressure from the prophecies of the Chronicles of Zornea-Hu, but that's no way to talk to guests. I think you know what you must do now."

The little man said, "Yes, Ms. Tiptip."

He looked at Steven and said, "I'm sorry."

You've heard of apologies that are said to be "dripping with insincerity"? Well, this one was so phony it had insincerity sloshing off of it like water barreling over the Kearsley Dam!

Ms. Tiptip continued, "And Steven, I know what you did was unintentional, but it's not enough to *try* to be considerate when you're in a new place or a new situation. You must be careful not to *unintentionally* hurt the feelings of others or be inconsiderate in any way. You must constantly be sensitive. Now, I think you know what you have to do."

Steven said, "Yes, Ms. Tiptip. I'm really sorry I slapped you off the table, sir."

The man said nothing, but his beady little holographic eyes burned into Steven.

Mr. Chickee said, "Fine. Now please continue, Horton. No one has to remind you that time is critical."

Horton once again bowed and repeated, "Welcome, one and all."

But guess who he didn't look at.

"I am Horton Flum-Flub, Holo-Explainer, the one whose responsibility it is to remove any questions you may have about Ourside and the current predicament in which we find ourselves.

"With your permission I will, by chronological age, flum-flub each of you, then set about removing your knowledge deficits.

"Ms. Cyrus-Herndon, I believe you are the oldest of our guests."

Richelle said, "Wait a minute, I'm not so sure about this. What in the world is flum-flubbing?"

Ms. Tiptip said, "I understand your reluctance, Richelle, but to flum-flub is to merely take a picture of certain bio-electrical energy patterns made by your brain. The patterns tell what it is you do or don't know about a particular subject, after which Horton puts together a program to bring you up to speed. Flum-flubbing simply identifies then erases your ignorance. It's designed to save time, it's the way all of our people in Ourside are educated. It's quite safe and painless and has no side effects other than enlightenment."

Richelle said, "What do I have to do?"

Ms. Tiptip said, "Simply give your permission."

Richelle said, "Okay, why not? Go ahead."

Horton hummed for exactly 2.8 seconds, then blew a puff of holographic air at Richelle. He said, "Finished. Steven, old chum, I believe you're next oldest."

Steven put his hand over his eyes so as not to look at Richelle and asked, "Can flum-flubbing get rid of this point zero one percent change that happened to me? And it's not going to hurt, is it?"

Richelle said, "Would you hurry up and give your permission, please! Look at me, does it seem like I was hurt? Flum-flubbing just feels like hummingbird wings brushing over your cheeks."

Steven said, "There's no way I'm looking at you again. All right, Mr. Holo-Explainer, you can do it."

Horton once again hummed for 2.8 seconds, shot another puff of holographic air in Steven's direction and said, "Finished. Russell?"

"This sounds fun! Fire away!"

"No. You must actually give your permission. 'Fire away' will not do."

Russell said, "Oops! Okay, you can flum-flub me."

Horton whooshed air at Russell.

"Finished."

Russell said, "Hey! How come you didn't hum before you finished me?"

Horton rolled his eyes and said, "The humming is done for nothing but show; we know how mysterious you Your-siders like to make everything. But if you insist, hmmmmm. Now one moment, please."

Horton closed his eyes, then said, "Finished. Please enjoy the presentation."

He seemed to fade until the tabletop was empty.

Then his voice could be heard, "Many uncounted years ago, not long after Ourside and Yourside were torn apart, the first porch, or doorway between the two worlds, was discovered."

From the table a bright flash exploded, then disappeared.

After blinking many times, the friends from Flint saw the image of a small porch standing on the table. Above the porch's doorway was printed ZORNEA-HU.

Russell pointed at the table and said, "That's so cool! How did they—"

Richelle and Steven each went, "Russell, shhh!"

Ms. Tiptip said, "No, no, children, it's all right. The Holo-Vision is designed to be interactive. Through many years of flum-flubbing we've recognized that one of the more beautiful things about having ignorance erased is that it leads to many more questions being asked. You discover that knowledge, instead of causing you to be satisfied with what you've learned, causes you to hunger for more and more knowledge."

Russell said, "Hey! That sounds like how I feel if I eat just one Triple Chocolate Double Butter Extra Sugared Candy Delight—I want more and more. Mmm! Like the commercial says, 'Obesity isn't such a bad price to pay after all.' "

Mr. Chickee said, "Well . . . it's *sort* of like that, Russell."

He blinked rapidly again, then said, "You know what? It's *nothing* at all like that. The more you know, the more you understand how little you actually know and the more you *want* to know. So the Holo-Vision takes this into consideration and allows any questions that may pop up in your mind to be asked and then answered. So it's fine to interrupt and ask anything. Go ahead, Russell."

Russell said, "Uh, I forgot what I was saying."

Horton said, "As *I* was saying, the porch to Zornea-Hu remained open only briefly, during which time the people from Ourside learned much about life from the woman who lived there. It was through her teachings and writings and guidance that we advanced so much more rapidly than the people of Yourside, who, some feel, unfortunately chose to follow other leaders."

Richelle said, "Excuse me, was this a real woman or was she a myth?"

Horton said, "She was real. We never knew her actual name, so we've always called her Zornea-Hu, which was, as you've seen, what's written above her door."

Richelle said, "Do you know anything more about her?"

"We only know she was born on Yourside in one of your states, called Florida."

A 3-D map of the United States appeared on the table and a small star glinted from northeast Florida.

"She's also recognized as being the first Old Soul."

The table was suddenly filled with twenty-seven soup-can-height people.

Russell said, "Hey! That's you and Ms. Tiptip, Mr. Chickee!"

"Yes, it is a representation of us."

The people waved and smiled at the Flint Future Detectives.

"Wow!" Russell said. "Can they see us?"

"Yes, the actual Old Souls are getting something very similar to what you call a voice mail and are responding."

Steven said, "If these are the *Old* Souls, how come some of them look so young? That one is a baby!"

Horton Flum-Flub Holo-Explainer said, "The name Old Soul refers not to their chronological age but to their spiritual age. The Old Souls are a group of people who have unusually high amounts of certain personality traits, things such as tolerance, open-mindedness, patience, acceptance and humility."

Russell whispered to Steven, "Sounds like the kind of people who never get invited to go anywhere."

Ms. Tiptip said, "We have those traits and are never satisfied with what we've learned, we always want to know more."

Russell whispered, "See, I told you, they're all party poopers."

Mr. Chickee said, "We also can feel the pain or joy that others feel."

Horton said, "As I said, Zornea-Hu was officially the first person we recognized with these traits. Sadly, she was never aware of her uniqueness. She was told so many times that she was 'peculiar' and 'difficult' and 'weird' and 'out of place,' that unfortunately toward the end she believed these things. We've since learned she was actually nothing more than an Old Soul."

On the table a woman dressed in old-fashioned clothes

could be seen sitting at a desk writing with one of those old typewriter thingies. She pulled the piece of paper that she'd been working on out of the typewriter, read it over, then, as her shoulders slumped, shook her head and wadded the paper into a ball.

Horton said, "She thought of her writings as whimsical little ditties done to relieve boredom and sorrow. She actually spent most of her adult life doing what she called 'scribbling tiny stories and tinier poems,' but we on Ourside have discovered that she was actually a channel of wisdom from beyond. That paper she just tossed out was what has come to be known as the first prophecy from the Chronicles of Zornea-Hu."

Richelle said, "But she balled it up and threw it away. How do you know what it said?"

Horton said, "Observe."

Everything on the table froze except the wadded-up piece of paper. It floated out of the wastebasket and became larger and larger until it was the size of an actual sheet of printer paper. Then it unwadded itself. Written very clearly on the paper was

> *From a side not Ours will come a child*
> *With thoughts so odd and mind so wild.*
> *Though the wise may feel this is not the one,*
> *It's the sole true sign that the End's begun.*
> *For though they've searched from pole to pole,*
> *The Answer shall come from this new Old Soul.*

Before Steven had a chance to say, "Huh? I don't get it," Horton said, "We believe this is the first of the prophecies that Zornea-Hu made. We think it is the second most important one. It foretells the upcoming destruction, or the End, of Ourside. Our best minds also feel that it tells about the arrival here of you three and how our only hope of finding the Answer to our survival rests with you."

Russell said, "She'da got booed off the *Def Poetry* show. Are all her poems as weird as that one?"

Horton said, "Weird? That's one of the easiest to understand. Check this one out."

A second piece of paper floated out of Zornea-Hu's wastebasket and unwadded itself. It read:

There'll then be a day when an instructor of play
Will search for the way to young children flay.
And though they will squirm and wiggle like worms,
He'll hunt them like germs around blue
*   pachyderms.*
They'll answer the call and one by one fall
And be plastered to walls by brown, rubbery balls.

Horton said, "We were hoping that one of you would be able to translate this one. Is it ringing any bells?"

Richelle looked from Steven to Russell and back.

Russell looked from Richelle to Steven and back.

Steven wisely looked from Russell to the floor in front of Richelle and back.

The Flint Future Detectives were a very confused-looking group.

Ms. Tiptip put her hand on Richelle's shoulder and said, "Don't worry. It may come to you later. You children are our only hope. Actually *one* of you is. Some of the other prophecies tell us that the only way for the End not to come is if a child from Yourside can translate the final unrevealed prophecy before"—she checked her own Oops-a-Daisy—"before this counts all the way down. We're fervently hoping one of you is the Yoursider who can translate the last prophecy and let us know what we have to do to save ourselves."

Russell said to Richelle and Steven, "I hope it's one of you guys. Saving a whole world sounds like a good way to get a bad bellyache."

Ms. Tiptip said, "You're right, Russell, it is a terrible burden to have placed on the shoulders of someone so young. However, that is what has happened and we can't change that."

Richelle said, "Well, give us this last prophecy and we'll see if one of us can read it. Then we can go find Rodney Rodent."

Ms. Tiptip said, "Ah, my dear, if only it were that simple."

Mr. Chickee said, "Unfortunately, we're not exactly certain where the last prophecy is. We do know that whoever the new Old Soul is, they'll have to complete a series of missions before the prophecy is revealed. All three of you shall be tested, and only one of you shall be the one. We won't know which of you is the Old Soul until you've returned from your missions."

Ms. Tiptip said, "That's not to say you're being forced to do this. The mission may be especially messy for one of you. So there's no reason you can't return to the porch, say the bow-yippee chant and go back to Flint right this minute. We want to be sure you realize you're under no obligation to help us."

Mr. Chickee said, "Which is why we want you to decide what you'll do. If any of you wants to leave, we'll understand, we'll hope whoever is left is the Old Soul. But we must tell you, if you do choose to stay, the missions will probably be very dangerous."

Richelle said, "Excuse me, Ms. Tiptip and Mr. Chickee, these boys and I need to have a meeting. This shouldn't take very long."

The adults walked a few feet away.

"I hereby call this special meeting of the Flint Future Detectives to order. As president, I move that we do everything we can to help Ourside, as long as it takes less than"—she looked at the countdown watch—"than twenty-nine days, twenty-three hours, thirty-one minutes and eighteen seconds."

Russell and Steven both said, "I second that emotion."

Richelle rolled her eyes.

They walked over to where Mr. Chickee and Ms. Tiptip were standing.

Richelle said, "We have a few questions. First, is it possible that we can have this done before the time on the Oops-a-Daisy runs out?"

Ms. Tiptip said, "I suppose anything is possible."

Russell said, "Now, when you say what we're gonna have to do is dangerous, is that *dangerous* with a capital *D* or a little *d*?"

Mr. Chickee said, "That all depends on the paths you take. Some paths have a danger rating of one and others have a danger rating of ten."

Russ asked, "What do those numbers mean?"

Ms. Tiptip said, "A danger rating of one is the amount of danger you'd be in if a raindrop fell on your head. A danger rating of ten is the trouble you'd be in if a ten-story building crashed into your forehead."

Richelle looked at Steven and Russell.

Russell looked at Richelle and Steven.

Steven forgot and looked at Russell and Richelle.

He found himself singing, "I'd go anywhere, for you, dear, anywhere, for you, dear, anywhere for you!"

Both Richelle and Russell balled their right fists.

Steven quickly looked away.

Richelle said, "It's unanimous, Ms. Tiptip and Mr. Chickee, the Flint Future Detectives are here to do anything we can."

Mr. Chickee smiled and said, "Was there ever any doubt?"

He handed Russell and Steven their own Oops-a-Daisies.

Richelle said, "Okay, what exactly do we have to do?"

Ms. Tiptip clapped twice and a large map the Holo-Vision. She said, "We believe your involves finding the one you call Rodney Ro here now." She pointed at a spot on the map wit

"And one of you needs to decide where you'll g certain areas I will serve as your guide, in others we shall hire someone else to lead you."

Russell pointed at a place where a door with two knobs was drawn.

"Here," he said, "I got a funny feeling in my gut that this is where we need to go."

Mr. Chickee and Ms. Tiptip gasped.

She said, "Oh, dear. Well, I'm afraid that's one of the areas that neither I nor Othello can travel in. What we'll do is show you how to get to a place where you can hire a guide who will take you there. The only thing I can tell you is do not pay the guide until you return safely from your journey."

Richelle said, "Won't all of this take too much time?" She tapped her Oops-a-Daisy. "I know a month seems long, but I've got a feeling these missions are going to take a lot longer down here than we think. Why do we need to hire a guide? Wouldn't it be quicker if we followed a map?"

Mr. Chickee said, "I'm afraid not, there are too many pitfalls and dangers involved in traveling in that area without a person who knows the way. Don't worry, though, the guides are a noble profession and are almost always wonderful people."

No one seemed to notice that Mr. Chickee had said

iost always wonderful people." I don't know about you, but I smell a rat.

He finished, "But you are right, Richelle, the sooner you get started the better. There might be complications along the way."

He wrote a set of numbers and dots on a piece of paper. "When you get to Guide Land, tell them this is where you need to go. Do you have any questions?"

Russell said, "What do they eat in Guide Land?"

Steven said, "Was that little holo-man serious about getting even with me?"

Richelle said, "Where is it exactly that this guide is going to lead us?"

Russell said, "What's a pitfall, is it sort of like a giant spitball?"

Steven said, "How mean is that holo-man for real?"

Richelle said, "Who'll tell us which is the Old Soul?"

Between all the whos and whys and whats and wheres and whens and hows, Mr. Chickee and Ms. Tiptip were swamped.

Finally she banged her walking staff on the ground and said, "Enough! I know this is overwhelming, but you do need to get started. We'll take you to another porch and you can enter Guide Land. As for your other questions, your dictionary has been downloaded with all the information you'll need. Just ask and it will help. But quickly, we must get you started."

She walked toward another porch, climbed the stairs

and said, "Here. Enter and begin your first mission. We'll be waiting."

Russell said, "Can't you come with us, Mr. Chickee?"

"No, Russell. You have to do this on your own. Besides, the land where you've chosen to go has a lot to do with Yourside. When I go there, I am sightless again. Please hurry, time is running out."

Russell, Richelle and Steven followed Ms. Tiptip onto the porch.

Steven said, "How do we get in? Do we have to say bow-wow . . ."

Ms. Tiptip said, "No, you just turn the knob and go on in."

Russell said, "But where do we go when we get in there?"

"Russell," Mr. Chickee said, "just like you had a feeling you were supposed to go to this particular area, you have to trust your feelings once you're inside, you have to follow your instincts."

Russell said, "Seems like it would be a lot easier if we had to follow a yellow brick road or something."

Richelle tapped her Oops-a-Daisy again, turned the doorknob and said, "Okay, Flint Future Detectives, time's a-wasting, let's go!"

They had started to walk into the door when Steven heard Horton Flum-Flub Holo-Explainer's voice in his ear.

"We have another old saying here in Holo-Land, 'Your chawda is rapawda and I'm the bazawda!' "

Steven flicked at his ear to get the annoying little

holo-sound out and said, "Dictionary, what does that mean?"

Great-great-grampa Carter's cranky dictionary said, "You really don't want to know. Let's just say it has something to do with grass and lawn mowers."

Steven followed Richelle and Russell through the porch door and thought, "Man, I hope things aren't any stranger in this next place!"

If that's what you're counting on, sorry 'bout your luck, Steven!

NINE

The Guide of Last Resort

ONCE THE FLINT FUTURE DETECTIVES walked through the door, they found themselves on another porch. There was no yellow brick road, but there was one street leading away from the porch, so they did what anybody would do, they followed it. The street led to a small grouping of houses.

Since he was a soon-to-be-great detective, Steven figured the house that they should go to first for information was the one that had a large sign out front that read: COME HERE FIRST FOR INFORMATION.

Richelle knocked twice on an ornately carved door.

Before her knuckle hit the wood a third time, an unpleasant voice yelled out, "What?" Then again, even louder, "WHA-A-A-T?"

Richelle said, "We're here to find out about hiring a

guide to take us to"—Richelle read from the paper Mr. Chickee had given her—"to sixteen dot dot, six dot, twenty-one dot, fourteen dot, eleven dot dot."

The door buzzed, then swung open.

They walked into a living room that had only a couch, a television and a thick book on a stand. On the wall of the room was a large Oops-a-Daisy that was counting down how much time was left for Ourside. Next to it was a sign that read, WELCOME TO THE HOUSE OF SULLEN GUIDES.

Underneath that someone had written with a blue crayon, YEAH, RIGHT!

Steven said, "Hello? Is anyone home?"

A teenage boy whose hair was braided walked into the room carrying a sandwich and a bag of salt-and-vinegar potato chips. Wires led from his pocket to a pair of earbuds. He plopped himself on the couch and used a remote to turn the television on.

After a full minute of watching the young man eat, Richelle put her hands on her hips, tapped her foot and said, "I can't believe how rude he is!"

Russell said, "Yeah, Mummy would have a great time straightening that guy out. She'd send him to Granny Forde in Jamaica in a second!"

Steven walked over to the teenager and tapped him on the shoulder. The kid brushed at his shoulder like a fly had landed there and never took his eyes off the television.

Richelle walked over to him, pulled the earbuds out and said, "Excuse me! Can't you see we need some help?"

The kid said, "So?"

Steven said, "Is there somebody in charge here?"

"In charge of what?"

"In charge of helping us find a guide."

The young man pointed at the book on the stand and said, "Check there."

Richelle, Russell and Steven walked over to the stand. On the page the book was opened to what appeared to be a list of people. They all seemed to have the same last name and most had the word OUT penciled in after their names:

Whitney Gruff-Guide OUT
Cydney Brusque-Guide VI OUT
Alexandra Abrupt-Guide III OUT
Hara Rude-Guide IX OUT
Shelby Curt-Guide IV OUT
Serena Churlish-Guide III OUT
Marian Short-Guide V OUT
Rebecca Impolite-Guide II OUT
Megann Hostile-Guide OUT
Enid Uncivil-Guide III OUT
Marvin Surly-Guide DXLI IN
Liz Gloomy-Guide IV OUT
Dali Dismal-Guide II OUT

Steven started turning pages, and each one was filled with names and Roman numerals. After every single name on all of the other pages was written OUT.

Russell said, "Bucko, let's ask the dictionary what this means. I don't think that grouchy old kid is going to tell us too much."

Steven looked at the thumb drive hanging around his neck.

"Man, I hate talking to this thing. But Dictionary, what's this all about?"

Great-great-grampa Carter's dictionary said, "Isn't it rather obvious? Many people in Ourside are named after the jobs they have. You are plainly in the house of one branch of the Guide family, and their job is to guide people throughout the land. What a shock!

"Using the reasoning powers of something like, oh let's be fair here, something like a large porous rock, I think it's pretty safe to assume that the ones with the word 'OUT' written after their name are probably not here, and the one with 'IN' is probably . . . go ahead, you're a future detective, you finish the sentence."

Russell piped up, "The one with 'IN' is probably here!"

Richelle said, "Dictionary, don't all of their last names mean just about the same thing?"

"Are you sure you're a member of this group? Your questions seem to have a flicker of intelligence in them. But you're right, they're all synonyms of the word 'sullen.' Hence the name on that sign, 'The House of Sullen Guides.' Looks like I'm going to have to rerank the intelligence of the Flint Future Detectives. You've gone right to the head of the class, young woman, surpassing the one who used to be the brightest in the club, that enormous, juicily salivating beast, Zoopy."

Steven rolled his eyes, looked at Richelle and couldn't help himself, he said, "Bright *and* beautiful, what more could a young brother ask?"

Both Russell and Richelle slapped Steven's head and said, "Look away!"

The kid on the couch said, "Oh, snap! That is the sickest thumb drive I've ever seen! I love its attitude, where did you get it?"

Richelle said, "Well! You do know how to hold a conversation after all."

"No, seriously, where did you get it?"

Russell said, "Let's make a deal. You tell us what we want to know and we'll tell you about the thumb drive."

"Bet! What do you want?"

Richelle pulled the paper from her pocket. "We need a guide to take us to . . . sixteen dot dot, six dot, twenty-one dot, fourteen dot, eleven dot dot."

The teenager said, "Easy! Even a pack of idiots like you could find that."

Richelle said, "That's it! I'm through with this place."

She marched to the front door and said, "Flint Future Detectives, let's go! Dictionary, you said this is the house of *one* branch of the Guide family, does that mean there are other Guides who aren't sullen and disrespectful and generally miserable?"

The dictionary said, "Wow! You *are* pretty bright! Correct again. There are—"

The teenager said, "Yeah, sure there are. There's the Tender Guides, the Loving Guides, the Merciful Guides, the Kindhearted Guides, the—"

Richelle said, "That's all we need to know. Thanks for nothing. Steven, Russell, let's go."

The kid said, "You're wasting your time. If you could read, you'd've seen that they're all out."

Richelle said, "Is that true, Dictionary?"

"True, like most of the people in this land, this young knucklehead is neither particularly bright nor exactly civil, but he, and the rest of the denizens of Guide Land, are generally very truthful."

"Whoa!" the teenager squealed. "You've gotta tell me where I can get one of these!"

Russell said, "How come all the other Guides are gone?"

The kid pointed at the Oops-a-Daisy on the wall.

Steven said, "What, they ran away because your world's going to be destroyed?"

"Of course not! Didn't you read the list, genius? There wasn't anyone there named Cowardly-Guide, was there? No one in the Guide family runs from anything, they're all gone because they've all been hired. It's your bad luck that for the first time in Ourside's history four thousand three hundred and twenty-two of the four thousand three hundred and twenty-three Guides have been hired at the same time."

Steven said, "Hired by who?"

"Oh, you think you're the only ones who want to leave? Your talking thumb drive was right, you aren't a real smart group, are you? Nearly everyone who has had some kind of contact with those bums from Yourside is trying to find a way to their world."

Russell said, "They're all trying to get to Earth?"

"Earth? Oh, I see now! You guys are Yoursiders! That explains why you're such morons." He frowned and said, "And that's where that cool thumb drive came from. You guys get all the cool toys there."

Richelle said, "Listen, there's one Guide that that list says is still in. We want to hire him."

The kid chuckled. "Oh, really? Don't you wonder why he's the only one who hasn't been hired?"

Steven said, "Yeah, I don't get it. If everyone's so desperate to get out of here, how come no one has chosen him?"

The dictionary said, "Word of warning, if you notice the number after the remaining Guide's name, you'll see it is five hundred and forty-one. That is a listing of how many generations his particular family has been guides."

Richelle said, "Oh, so does that mean since he's got so much experience he's too expensive to hire?"

The kid laughed. "Nope. We all cost the same."

Steven said, "Then why hasn't anyone taken him?"

Great-great-grampa Carter's dictionary said, "Not only is his family extremely experienced at guiding, they've also had many, many years of practicing being obnoxious and sullen and surly. I'm afraid he's still here because nobody can put up with his attitude."

Richelle said to the teenager, "What about you? Can't you guide us?"

The kid said, "Me? You think I'm one of the Sullen Guides?"

Russell said, "Sure, you're pretty mean. Is everybody in Ourside so hard to get along with?"

The teenager said, "Not at all. There are some folks here who are quite pleasant, but I stay away from them, I wouldn't want any of that niceness rubbing off on me."

Russell said, "Yeah, Mummy always tells me if you run around with dogs, you end up with fleas. Or is it if you run around with hogs, you end up with cheese? Or maybe it was if you roll around on logs, you end up—"

Richelle said, "Russell! Please! Time's wasting and we've got to get to this place."

She turned to the sullen teenager. "All right, we'll take the last Guide, whoever he is. How do we do it?"

The kid smiled and said, "Believe me, it'll be my pleasure to introduce you to Mr. Marvin Surly-Guide, I'll go get him."

He walked out of the room and it sounded like he banged a bunch of pots and pans together. A second later he walked back in.

He said, "Morons from Yourside, I'd like to introduce you to the most wonderful of the Sullen Guides, the most intelligent, the most well-loved and also the handsomest of all of the Guides!"

The Flint Future Detectives waited and watched the doorway that the kid had just walked through.

Finally Richelle said, "Well?"

The teenager said, "Well what?"

"Well, where is he?"

"Right here! It's me!"

Richelle's eyes rolled. "Are you kidding?"

The teenager said, "When I said 'the handsomest of all of the Guides,' it should've been a dead giveaway. Sort of like asking, what color is the little brown jug?"

Russell said, "Wait! Wait! Don't tell me!"

Richelle groaned and said, "I guess we have no choice. Let me explain, we're the Flint Future Detectives and we'd like to hire you to take us to—"

The kid bellowed, "I know, I know. Why do you want to go there? All the other saps are trying to get to Yourside."

Russell stepped behind Steven and said, "Mr. Chickee said I should follow my feelings and that's where I feel we should go."

The kid said, "Mr. Chickee? Othello Chickee sent you? Why didn't you say so?"

Steven and Richelle sighed and smiled. Richelle said, "We didn't know it would make a difference."

The boy yelled, "It doesn't! But rules are rules, and if Othello Chickee's involved, it means that Ms. Tiptip and a ton of other Old Souls are too, so it looks like I haven't got any choice, I've got to take you. How much time is left on your Oops-a-Daisy?"

Richelle checked her wrist. "Oh, no! We're already

down to twenty-nine days, twenty-three hours, nineteen minutes and fifty-two seconds!"

Marvin Surly-Guide said, "I can't believe it. It's always me who gets involved in things like this. Listen, I don't know if you have time enough to get there and back. Don't know and don't care. But if you're going to have any kind of chance, we've got to get going. It always takes a lot longer to get there and back than you think it will."

Russell said, "We're ready!"

Marvin said, "Then let's go. The porch we need isn't far, but judging by the way you guys look and act, leading you clowns is going to be as hard as leading a herd of cats."

Great-great-grampa Carter's dictionary said, "Oh joy, not only is he arrogant, surly and obnoxious, this charmer is also blessed with impatience."

Marvin said, "Wow! That thing is so sick! We're going to have to work something out so that if I get you guys back here safe you'll give him to me."

Richelle said, "Whatever, but time is wasting, we need to go."

TEN

The Journey to H.A.L.F. Land

IT DIDN'T TAKE LONG to see why no one from Ourside had wanted to hire Marvin Surly-Guide. He was doing his job, but just barely. He was horrible at the Guide part of his name and absolutely great at the Surly part.

He wasn't telling the Flint Future Detectives much more than "Turn here" or "Can't you walk any faster?" or "If I was you, I wouldn't touch that." (Which he didn't say until Russell had tried to eat something he found that was brown and gooey and smelled like corn bread, something that right after he took a bite bit him right back.)

Any questions Steven and Richelle and Russell asked were ignored or met with a roll of the eyes or a rude snort.

But it was Russell who finally seemed to get the guide's attention.

"Hey, how come we haven't seen any cute, teeny trolls with hair growing out of their ears or from between their toes? Every book I've ever read where people go to a strange world and take a journey there're always a bunch of trolls that come out to make them laugh. Seems like we've been walking long enough that we should've run into one or two by now. And I could use a good laugh."

Marvin gave a small shudder and said, "Don't worry, there are plenty of hairy, tiny people where we're headed. Not very many of them are cute, though. Mostly they're irritating, goofy little twits. Sort of like smaller, older versions of you guys.

"I feel bad about you getting bit by that barfoodle, so I'm gonna give you one word of warning about those little people, kid. When we do run into one, they don't like it when anyone calls them trolls, they wanna be called Whizzers."

Russell got his laugh. He put his hand over his mouth and said, "You said 'whizzers'!"

Great-great-grampa Carter's dictionary said, "No, Russell. As defined in *The Dictionary of Modern Ourside: Whizzer* ([WHIZ-ur] n. *Any of a race of diminutive, incomplete, trouble-causing, supernatural beings exiled from Yourside, found almost exclusively inhabiting various rooms in the H.A.L.F. Land sector of Ourside.*)"

Marvin said, "Your talking book hit the nail right on the head."

Russell said, "These Whizzers are troublemakers?"

"Of course they are, but don't worry about running into them out here, they're kept just about on lockdown."

Richelle, Steven and Russell all said, *"Kept?"*

"Ooh, touchy little bunch of Yoursiders, aren't we? Yes, they're kept, but no, it's not like they're prisoners or slaves or anything. Nearly everyone you'll run into where we're going stays in different rooms and they're cool with it. They can jet whenever they want, but most of 'em just chill in their rooms."

Richelle said, "Okay, Surly-Guide, I'm not taking one more step until you tell us where we're headed. This place doesn't sound like somewhere I want to go."

Marvin turned his nose up at Richelle and said, "It's the place your cool talking book said, H.A.L.F. Land."

"Halfland?"

"H.A.L.F. Land, two words. The initials stand for the Hopeless, Abandoned, Lost and Forgotten."

Russell said, "No! I'm not going back to Flint until I find Rodney Rodent!"

Marvin said, "No, not Flint."

Richelle said, "Russell, stop! Marvin, you're talking about a land where people are separated because they're hopeless and lost? This place is sounding worse by the minute! I'm turning right around and going back to Mr. Chickee and Ms. Tiptip! I can't believe they'd let us go somewhere like that."

"Nice speech, Miss Cyrus-Herndon. Let's all wait a minute and see if it's made me cry . . . nope. But if you could stop being Miss High-and-Mighty for a second, you'd see there's nothing fishy going on." Marvin snorted. "People here in Ourside *would* find it strange that someone from Yourside has a problem with H.A.L.F. Land, though."

Richelle said, "Why? You should stop stereotyping, some of us from Earth are very compassionate."

"You think so, huh? Still, some folks in Ourside would think it's weird you're worried, because everyone and everything in H.A.L.F. Land is there because of something a bunch of people from your Earth did."

Richelle said, "What?"

"Yeah. And these Earth people don't send only Whizzers to H.A.L.F. Land either, they send all kinds of characters. The old folks in Ourside have tried to make the Yoursiders stop sending these Whizzers and things here, but they keep on disrespecting us and acting like they don't care. They're a real hardheaded group of people."

Russell said, "They sound like a bunch of losers, who are they?"

"You're right, they're some *real* losers. Your people call them things like authors, playwrights, poets."

Richelle said, "They're writers?"

"Yeah, that's them, *writers.*" Just saying the word made him twist his face like he was having a seventy-two-bean-burrito bellyache.

"The old folks here have been trying to let them know they need to quit sending us the hopeless, the abandoned, the lost and the forgotten, but more and more of them come. And since Yourside discovered word processors and computers, we get tons of them every day."

Steven said, "Huh? I don't get it. My mom said most authors don't make enough money to send a letter across town, much less send someone to another world."

"That's just it, they don't get charged anything to send these characters to us." The guide seemed to remember he was trying hard to be uncooperative. "Look, I'm a Guide, not an Explainer, not a Decider. There's a sign outside of H.A.L.F. Land that'll tell you how everyone and everything there got in."

Richelle scrunched her left eye partially shut and left her right eye partially open. She twisted her lips to the right, then back to the left. "You've got horrible manners, but you haven't misled us so far, so I guess we'll keep going."

Marvin gasped and said, "My word! If I were to mislead you even one time, I'd lose my license! My family has been honorable Guides for five hundred and forty-one generations. I don't intend to do anything to break that string. I just wish I had a higher-class group of people to deal with."

A house near a large tree appeared around a bend in the road. A sign hung from the front of the porch:

WELCOME TO THE PORCH TO H.A.L.F. LAND.

*TO GAIN ENTRY YOU MUST BE A FICTIONAL CHARACTER IN A PLAY, STORY, NOVEL, SONG, OR POEM WRITTEN OR CREATED BY A YOURSIDER.

*YOU MUST BE NEITHER FULLY COMPLETED NOR USED IN ANY OF YOUR WRITER/CREATOR'S FINISHED WRITING.

*YOU ARE ALSO WELCOME IF YOUR WRITER/CREATOR WANTED TO USE YOU BUT HASN'T WITHIN THE PAST NINE MONTHS.

*YOU ARE WELCOME TO LIVE HERE AS LONG AS YOU'D LIKE, BUT ONCE YOUR WRITER/CREATOR PUTS YOU INTO A COMPLETE STORY, YOU MUST IMMEDIATELY LEAVE H.A.L.F. LAND. IF YOU'RE LUCKY, YOU WILL THEN BE INDUCTED INTO C.O.I.L. LAND.

*OTHER PEOPLE CAN ENTER IF THEY ARE IN THE PRESENCE OF A MEMBER OF THE GUIDE FAMILY.

Russell said, "I get it! If some writer uses their imagination to come up with a person in a story and doesn't finish writing the story, instead of floating around in space or being trapped in a computer or on some paper, that pretend person gets to come here and live!"

Marvin said, "That's right, partner, except it's not only people. To get into H.A.L.F. Land or C.O.I.L. Land it can also be an animal, real or fake, or a place or a thing."

Richelle said, "So, what is this C.O.I.L. Land?"

"Some more initials, they stand for Capable of Infinite Life. It's where only the greatest characters go."

Great-great-grampa Carter's dictionary said, "It's like this. A completely drawn character in a book has the ability to live forever. Not many of Earth's literary characters are worth remembering beyond two or three decades, after which they must leave C.O.I.L. Land and go back to the books they were created for. An extremely small group is still discussed and thought about centuries after their creation. In all of Yourside's written history there have been only several dozen who're more or less permanent residents of C.O.I.L. Land."

Richelle said, "Wow! If we have time, that's the place we should go. I'd rather meet some of the characters from my favorite books instead of some people who are just bits and parts of authors' dreams and imaginations."

Marvin said, "Common mistake, but what else could I expect from a common little girl? You *really* don't want to go there. There's nothing that messes with you Yoursiders' minds more than finally meeting a book character you've thought was so, so wonderful. Then when you find out they are nothing but a total . . . oh dear, what is the word you Yoursiders use? Here we call them obnoxious scumquats, but I can't remember your term. Talking Book, what's the word I wanna use?"

Great-great-grampa Carter's dictionary said, "The closest translation would be *jerk* ([*JURK*] n. *Slang. A person regarded as disagreeable, contemptible, etc., especially as the result of mean or foolish behavior*). Hey! That's a pretty accurate description of you."

"Oh, man! I've just gotta get me one of these thumb drives!"

Richelle said, "Wait a minute, why in the world would great characters from books be jerks?"

The dictionary said, "I'm sure you've read a book where the characters in it seem so real that you can talk to them; that's because the author has done such a marvelous job that those characters not only seem real, they become real. They live. And just like any living person who is adored and worshipped and loved for no apparently deserved reason—think of most of your politicians, professional athletes and pop music stars—they have a tendency to become very full of themselves."

Marvin said, "Yeah, some people here call you guys from Earth Your-o-trash! The talking book is right, but let me break it down for you. Have any of you read one of your Earth books called *The Odyssey?*"

Russell looked away from the surly teenager, the way any really smart student does whenever their teacher has asked a question they don't know the answer to. Steven looked away too. He told himself, "Now not only do I have to not look at Richelle, I've got to stop looking at this surly guide if he's gonna start asking a bunch of embarrassing questions!"

Richelle said, "Of course I've read it, it's about Odysseus and his search to come back home."

"Right. Well, let me tell you, he's the king of jerks! He's fighting to have a holiday named in his honor.

"And how about a book called *Moby-Dick?*"

Russell looked at his fingernails, Steven checked out the sky.

Richelle said, "Yes."

"That Captain Ahab guy? What a loser! He is so obnoxious that he's been made an honorary member of the Sullen Guide family, but I'm going to tell you, not even any of us can stand him!

"But enough chitchat, are you ready to enter H.A.L.F. Land?"

Each one of the Flint Future Detectives tried to look brave. Madam President said, "We're ready."

The only thing Steven and Russell could do was go, GULP!

ELEVEN

You Must Be Hairy Plodder's Mummy!

THE GROUP OF FOUR OPENED THE DOOR and walked through. The way the Flint Future Detectives had gone in was right in front of a door that read, BOWLING, B. T. To the right as far as you could see ran jillions of other doors with two knobs that looked exactly the same. To the left as far as you dared look were more double-knobbed doors than you could believe!

"Wow!" Richelle said.

"Man!" Steven said.

"Ooo-whee!" Russell said.

Great-great-grampa Carter's dictionary said, "According to my information, to enter a particular author's county you must first turn the knob on the left halfway to the right, the knob on the right three-quarters of the way to the left. You then must pause three point two seconds, knock three and a half times, and look through the peephole and await permission to enter."

Steven said, "Can't we stop talking and look in one of these rooms?"

Russell said, "Yeah, I want this one. Isn't B. T. Bowling the woman who wrote the Hairy Plodder books? She's one of my favorite writers, I want to see what's behind her door. I bet there're skillions of trol—oops . . . skillions of Whizzers and creatures and things!"

Steven turned the left-hand knob halfway to the right and the right-hand knob three-quarters of the way to the left, waited exactly three point two seconds, knocked three and a half times (a very difficult thing to do, try it. No, seriously, try it. See? Not as easy to do as it sounds, is it?), then looked through the peephole.

A voice with an English accent called, "One moment, please."

Richelle said, "Who is it that's going to open the door?"

Marvin said, "Oh, that would be the Earth writer who made up the characters in the room, her name's B. T. Bowling. Every time your writers send another character here, they also have to give a part of their spirit too, to stay with their creations. The old folks hope if writers keep losing parts of their spirit, maybe they'll become frustrated and quit writing."

The door swung up and the group stepped into a room that was around a mile deep and two miles wide with a ceiling that was half a mile up. Right in the middle of the room was what looked like a great big aboveground swimming pool with a cover over the top of it.

On the left-hand side of the room stood fifty of the biggest dump trucks anyone had ever seen. But the only person or character or thing that was standing in the room was a woman who had her back turned to them.

Steven whispered to Russell, "I guess when you write books that are a thousand pages long, there aren't too many characters left over to send here."

The woman turned around. "Welcome! It's so good to see people from Earth!"

Russell said, "Wow! You must be Hairy Plodder's mummy!"

The woman said, "I've never heard it expressed so peculiarly before, but I suppose that, yes, I am the one who gave him life."

Marvin and the Flint Future Detectives introduced themselves, and Russell said, "Excuse me, Ms. Bowling, how come there's no one else in your room?"

B. T. Bowling said, "But there *is* someone else." She pointed up and everyone in the room gasped, for flying along the very top of the room was a most magnificent winged beast!

Ms. Bowling said, "That's the Great Morose Fire-Spewing Clabbernabber."

And this animal was great indeed!

Imagine the graceful way a dolphin moves in the ocean,

think of how the water seems to let it pass without the slightest notice, much in the same way a thought slips effortlessly through your mind, that's how smoothly, how easily, this enormous dragon sailed through the air.

And my, how its wings moved!

Strength and power shimmered through the Great Morose Fire-Spewing Clabbernabber as each flexion of the thick muscles that ran the length of both of its wings brushed and stroked the air so rhythmically that the animal seemed to be dancing with the wind instead of flying through it.

Tucked tightly into its faintly reptilian belly the Flint Future Detectives could see bright yellow talons that wouldn't have been out of place on an eagle the size of a jumbo jet, each joint, each segment, looking as if it had been cast out of pure gold, each of its ten claws ending in spikes that sparkled as if molded from diamonds.

And the tail of the beast was horrific!

It was tri-pronged and whipped like a flag in the wind. Where it came to an end bolts of purplish lightning leapt and sparked and crackled between its three glowing tips.

But the most amazing thing about the Clabbernabber was its head!

No one in the room, not Richelle, not Steven, not Russell, not Marvin, not Ms. Bowling herself, could look at the head for more than a second. Anytime their gaze landed on the beast's head, something very basic, very primordial caused their eyes to slide away and down. Something about the inky, swirling blackness of the eyes of the animal wouldn't allow more than the quickest of glimpses to be stolen.

Or, as Russell said, "This is one bad mamma jamma *here*, boy! And look at those claws! He's got bling-bling for days!"

Ms. Bowling said, "Actually she's a female."

She snapped her fingers and the beast turned and dropped from the sky, landing several feet from her. When she touched down, a shudder ran through the floor of the room. As she folded her beautifully iridescent, humming-bird-colored wings into her sides, a gust of wind brushed past the detectives; it smelled strongly of warm cinnamon toast and butter. Once the animal settled down, Richelle figured she was at least fifteen feet tall.

Steven said, "I don't get it. That's the most amazing thing I've ever seen! Why haven't you used her in any of your books, Ms. Bowling?"

She sighed and said, "Yes, she is quite a creation, but unfortunately I haven't been able to use her because of one tragic flaw."

Russell shot a quick look at the mouth of the Clabbernabber. He couldn't keep his eyes on it long enough to decide if the mouth was shaped more like an alligator's or a crocodile's, but it was huge and bristling with two-inch-long yellow-streaked teeth.

He said to Ms. Bowling, "I know why you couldn't use her, she would have ate Hairy Plodder up in the very first book."

Ms. Bowling laughed. "No, she's a vegetarian, but it *is* because of what she eats that I haven't been able to find a way to use her."

Steven said, "Huh? I don't get it."

Ms. Bowling said, "The Great Morose Fire-Spewing Clabbernabber has a very limited diet. The only things she will eat are vegetables that begin with the letter *b*, which pretty well limits her to eating Brussels sprouts, broccoli and Boston baked beans. I know, there are beets and butternut squash, but she has no taste for them at all."

Marvin said, "Whoa, Ms. Yourside-Author, that's the second time you said that creature was a fire spewer. I don't know about these idiots, but I'm moving away from the mouth of this monster."

Ms. Bowling said, "This is really most embarrassing, but I can assure you that the safest place to stand is up here near her head. Let me demonstrate."

She clapped her hands twice and the cover over the pool started to pull away. It *was* a swimming pool, but instead of water it was filled with tons and tons of broccoli and Brussels sprouts floating on millions of gallons of Boston baked beans.

Everyone said, "Yuck!"

But the Clabbernabber filled the air with the cinnamon-toast-and-melting-butter aroma when it released a tremendous roar and half jumped, half flew to the edge of the pool. Using its golden, diamond-tipped talons to securely grab the pool's sides, it ducked its head into the nasty-looking mess and scarfed massive quantities of the noxious mixture.

It ate so ferociously that a little cloud of vaporized broccoli, Brussels sprouts and Boston baked beans hung over the pool.

After a few minutes of this *b* vegetable massacre Ms. Bowling snapped her fingers and the Clabbernabber leapt back to her side.

Steven said, "I still don't get it. You can't use her in your books just because she has real bad table manners and wants to eat that nasty vegetable junk?"

Ms. Bowling said, "That's the first part of the reason, unfortunately that's the least offensive part."

Russell was getting more and more familiar and comfortable around the Great Clabbernabber. While he still couldn't bring himself to look at the animal's head for more than a few seconds, he started giving its body a closer examination. He walked around to get a look at the electrified tail.

Ms. Bowling said, "Young man, I'd strongly recommend you not go back there this soon after she has eaten. You'd be wise to come back with us.

"The reason I can't use her in my books is because all of the *b* vegetables seem to make the poor girl become very flatulent and—"

Russell said, "Make her what?"

Great-great-grampa Carter's dictionary said, "Flatulent (*[FLACH-uh-lent] adj. Generating gas in the stomach or intestines, suffering from such an accumulation of such gas*)."

Ms. Bowling said, "Correct, and unfortunately when she passes gas . . ."

Russell laughed, put his hand over his mouth and said, "You said 'passes gas'!"

Steven said, "You don't have to explain anything else. I bet when something that big and rough-looking farts, the smell could fry a rhinoceros!"

Russell laughed again, kept his hand over his mouth and said, "Bucko, you said, 'farts'!"

Ms. Bowling said, "No, actually the smell is quite pleasant, it's the fact that the Clabbernabber has an open flame near . . ."

Before Ms. Bowling could say anything more the Clabbernabber's wings lurched forward and a great rumbling rolled from her belly.

Russell used his fingers to plug his ears and said, "Uh-oh, she's gonna burp!"

Steven used his fingers to plug his nose and said, "I doe tink zo, I tink she's gedding ready to cut a big . . ."

Steven was right, and the second the Clabbernabber's gas reached the sparking lightning bolts on her tail, a blue and green flame roared out and shot thirty feet behind her. The temperature in the room instantly rose twenty degrees!

"Wow!" all the members of the Flint Future Detectives and Marvin said at once.

Ms. Bowling said, "I know. So as you can see, the poor girl has proven to be quite impractical for any of Hairy's adventures. Forests, castles, caves, anything she was in would be instantly incinerated."

In no time at all three more flames jumped from the back of the Great Morose Fire-Spewing Clabbernabber.

Richelle wiped her brow and said, "Ms. Bowling, we have to go, but before we do, I was wondering, why weren't you able to use those dump trucks in any of your stories. Do they have a terrible flaw too?"

"Oh, *those*. Another large embarrassment, I'm afraid. Actually those aren't mine, they're from Earth and they come every hour on the hour."

Ms. Bowling looked at her watch and said, "I know you're pressed for time, but if you can wait for just a moment more, you'll see why they're here."

A second later a whistle blew and the engines of the fifty dump trucks roared to life and one hundred headlights came on.

Steven looked at the Clabbernabber. Richelle was standing next to her and petting her nose! In the one or two seconds that he could actually look at the mighty dragon's head Steven wasn't sure if her nose looked like an elephant's or a lion's, but whatever it was, Richelle's hands were rubbing back and forth across it and the beast's inky black eyes were shut! The "Oooga-ooga-ooga" sound the Clabbernabber was making reminded Steven of purring.

The dump trucks started coming toward them.

Richelle scratched at the Clabbernabber's ear and said, "Hold on a minute, sweetie, fresh food is just about here."

Ms. Bowling said, "No, Richelle, it's not food that the trucks are bringing."

The first dump truck reached the group and swung around so that its rear was facing them. A loud beep came just as the bed of the truck began to raise and the rear door yawned open.

Right at Ms. Bowling's feet, out poured an ocean of money! Skillions and jillions of green bills tumbled out of the bed of the truck!

Richelle picked one of them up, laughed and said, "For a second there I thought this was real American money. What do you do with all of this counterfeit cash, Ms. Bowling?"

Ms. Bowling said, "No, child, this is real."

Richelle squinched her right eye halfway shut and left her left eye halfway open. She twisted her lips to the left, then to the right, and gave the bill a closer look.

She put her hand on her hip and said, "I'm sorry to have to tell you this, Ms. Bowling, but this is *not* real money. There has never been a president or founder of the United States named HWMISB. There aren't even enough vowels in that word for it to be a real name."

Russell picked one of the bills up and said, "Uh-oh, Madam President, I hate to be the one who's got to burp your bubble, but these *are* real. Bucko."

He handed the bill to Steven.

Steven felt the room start to spin and it wasn't caused only by the farting of the Clabbernabber. Looking out at him from the face of the bill in his hand was a very sweaty, tired-looking man who seemed to be having both a bad hair day and a very bad stomachache. Yup, it was the hardest-working man in show business, the Godfather of Soul, Mr. James Brown! The dump trucks were filled with . . .

Russell and Steven cried out at the same time, "Quadrillion-dollar bills!"

"My word!" Ms. Bowling said. "How in heaven's name did you know the proper name for those? I'd been told they were an absolute secret back on Earth!"

Russell said, "You wouldn't believe how much trouble those things can get you in!"

Steven said, "All fifty of those trucks are filled with quadrillion-dollar bills?"

Ms. Bowling said, "As I said, it's a tad embarrassing, but this is how I get paid for my writing."

Steven said, "Huh? I don't get it."

Richelle let out a tiny growl.

Ms. Bowling said, "People from America have bought so many of my Hairy Plodder novels, and the tastefully done spin-off items that are associated with them, that if the publishing company were to pay me what I've earned, every piece of paper currency that your country has ever printed since 1779 would now be mine.

"This is top-secret, but to give me my royalties your Treasury Department had to create and print nine septillion of these quadrillion-dollar bills, which allows me to get paid and still leaves enough cash for your fellow American citizens to use for their day-to-day expenses. You know, buying hamburgers and gasoline and ammunition and such things."

Russell said, "Well, Bucko, I guess that's why Ms. Tiptip said we didn't all-the-way solve the mystery of the quadrillion-dollar bill!"

Before Steven could answer, the Clabbernabber started ooga-ooga-ing again, and with each ooga she shot a hot blue flame thirty feet behind her.

Richelle said, "Goodness! I've got to stop petting you now, sweetie. You're really warming the room up!"

She turned to the author and said, "Ms. Bowling, we'd love to talk some more, but we've got work to do."

Ms. Bowling said, "It's really most extraordinary the way she lets you pet her, but I agree, you should leave. It's getting intolerably warm in here!"

The Flint Future Detectives, Marvin, and Ms. Bowling shook hands and wished each other luck. Steven turned the left-hand knob on the door to the right and the right-hand knob to the left, and the door rose and let them out.

Before the door shut, Richelle called back to the Clabbernabber, "See you later, sweetie!"

Steven said, "Not in this lifetime you won't, that's one scary animal!"

Russell said, "Yeah, Madam President, why are you calling that dragon 'sweetie'?"

"She kind of reminds me of me, she is sweet and no one really understands her."

Steven's eyes rolled and he said, "Mr. Surly-Guide, do we have time to visit any other authors?"

Marvin looked at his Oops-a-Daisy and said, "Hey, it's your lives, you think I care if ninety-nine years go by on . . ."

Russell ran farther up the hallway, heading toward the A doors. He stopped at one door and read:

BUSTER B. BAYLISS COUNTY
IT IS HIGHLY RECOMMENDED THAT YOU GO SOMEWHERE ELSE. BUT
IF YOU INSIST ON ENTERING, IT WOULD BE SMART
IF YOU HAD:
a pair of hair clippers
a good sense of humor
a great life insurance policy
a thick skin
a book of waterproof matches
a bottle of Old Spice aftershave

Russell hollered back, "Look, I know who this is! He's the guy who writes those cool Ben-Jammin, the Baddest Barber and Outdoor Adventure Brother, books."

Steven said, "Ben-who?"

"Oh, man, Bucko, I can't believe you haven't read any of the Ben-Jammin stories. He's that guy who's cutting hair until he saves enough money to follow his dream to be the world's greatest outdoor adventurer."

Richelle's arms crossed and her foot started tapping. "Come on, Russell, thirty-two quadrillion authors here and this is the one you're interested in, someone who writes about an outdoor adventure barber?"

Russell had two ways of dealing with people who were negative: he either ignored them or pretended he didn't hear them. He decided to do the ignoring way with Richelle.

He turned the left-hand knob on the door halfway to the

right and the right-hand knob three-quarters of the way to the left, waited three point two seconds, knocked three and a half times (go ahead, try it again, keep practicing!), and stood on his tiptoes to look through the peephole.

A gruff, outdoorsy voice yelled, "Who is it?"

Russell said, "Someone who's ready to go on a wilderness adventure, let me in, please."

The door flew up.

Marvin looked back and screamed out, "No! Stop him! Not there! That's Buster B. Bayliss County!"

The guide rushed toward the door Russell was standing in front of. He was absolutely panicked and screamed, "No! Stop now, you little idiot!"

But Russell stepped in and the door shut behind him.

The guide pulled at his hair and said, "Aww, man, that little sap just went in the most dangerous county in all of H.A.L.F. Land! And it'll be my fault if anything happens to him."

Steven said, "Hurry up! Let's open the door and go get him."

The guide slumped against the door and said, "We can't."

Richelle said, "Why not?"

"The only way the door can be opened before a week has gone by is if that knucklehead opens it from inside, and what do you bet he isn't going to want to?"

Steven said, "Why wouldn't he?"

"Weren't you listening to me? It's a dangerous place,

boys love danger, he'll have a great time. If he isn't ripped to shreds and eaten."

Steven and Richelle yelled, "What?"

"Yeah, there's been this monster-bear thing on the loose in there for the longest time. It's eating anything that moves. And it loves fresh Yourside meat."

Steven tried like mad to open the door the way the dictionary had told him; nothing happened.

"Quit wasting your time. All of you Yoursiders are so selfish! Here I'm about to get into a ton of trouble and all you can think about is your foolish friend."

Richelle said, "Are you kidding? Russell might get killed and you're worried about getting in trouble? What can we do?"

The kid tapped his Oops-a-Daisy and said, "All we can do is pull up a chair and wait. If your bonehead friend doesn't open the door himself, we can go inside in a week and get what's left of him. Maybe if we find a bone or two, I won't get punished too bad."

Richelle looked at Steven.

Steven was so disturbed he looked right back at Richelle.

He said, "I can't believe Russell's in so much trouble, and Richelle, I can't believe it, but 'your love is all I nee-ee-ee-d, all I need, woo-oow-woo-woo-oow-woo, all I need!' "

Richelle slumped down next to the surly guide and said, "Carter, if you look at me even once during the next week, I'll make you wish *you* were trapped in Buster B. Bayliss County!"

Steven looked at his Oops-a-Daisy and said, "Don't worry, the only thing I'm going to look at for the next week is that door. The only thing I'm going to do for the next week is hope Russell opens it up from inside."

Marvin said, "I wouldn't hold my breath, that kid's probably already been eaten. And as greedy as that bear thing is, I bet he's already burped your partner's bones out."

TWELVE

The Return of Rodney Rodent

THE DOOR DROPPED behind Russell. What he saw crashed into his senses like a cheap-shot punch from a 360-pound lumberjack. To his right was a thick, impenetrable wall of green, running forty, maybe fifty feet up. A forest so dense and hot that it shimmered and danced as waves of heat and humidity rose from it.

To Russell's left was another wall, this one running as far up as he could see. Instead of the vibrant green of the first wall, this one was bright white. White from the blizzard of snow, hail and wind that tore through the area, making it just as impenetrable as the forest to the right.

Running between these two walls was a twenty-seven-foot-wide, calm and peaceful, grass-covered street.

Once the shock of what he was seeing wore off, something

even more disturbing came at Russell. From the left came the piercing howl of wind-whipped snow. Having been born and raised in Flint, Russell recognized what this sound was. It was the desperate, lonely sound of life in hiding, of life scoured and scourged into retreat and surrender by un-remitting cold and blasting winds.

From the right came a sound found only in the thickest jungles of sub-Saharan Africa or the densest rain forests of Brazil or the deepest woods of northern Canada. It was the sound of nature at its most horrifying. It was the crushing noise of unexpected violent attack, the wail of uncountable millions of life-or-death battles being fought. It was teeth and claws and stingers and jaws and talons and ambushes and fear. It was the scream of eat-or-be-eaten, it was the sound of life in the wild, the sound of life run amok.

Russell gasped and tried to protect himself by using his hands to cover his ears. Even then the sounds that pounded into his brain were horrifying.

Not in the sense of bad-scary-movie-at-the-mall horrify-ing, more in the way you'd be horrified if you got an invita-tion to go to the Hungry Crocodile Café and found out the only thing on the menu was a picture of y-o-u.

From all of this noise a familiar sound worked its way into Russell's mind, a sound that caused his very soul to be seized by a sense of panic.

And not the good, fun kind of panic either.

The sound was dogs charging in his direction from somewhere unseen.

The sound brought back a horrible memory, a memory that anyone who has ever been viciously attacked by a pack of hungry dogs can never forget.

Russell was positive this was the same sound that that roaming pack of Chihuahuas had made when they'd attacked him outside of Halo Burger last fall! Weren't those the same terrifying yips and yaps he'd heard when those vicious little curs had stood on each other's backs and snatched the bag holding his fish sandwiches deluxe with heavy tartar sauce from his suddenly useless hands?

Russell knew he didn't have time to think, knew if he didn't act immediately he would be swarmed again, swarmed and used. Used by a vicious pack of Chihuahuas.

He began acting on instinct. If you had asked him to put into words what was happening in his mind, he wouldn't have been able to, but somehow he knew he was getting messages and information from a place deep inside of him, a place long forgotten and unexplored.

Messages began taking shape in his mind that came from beyond his mother or his father, beyond even his father's ancestors in Jamaica or his mother's in Flint. This information must have been coming from a wise elder who had ruled in some ancient corner of the motherland.

And without thinking, Russell knew what to do.

And he did it.

Like a round stone dropped into a bucket of clear, cold water, he fell to the ground in a ball, wrapped his arms around his head and, sounding an awful lot like the hardest-working man in show business, began wailing, "Please, please, please, not again! Not the Chihuahuas!"

But the wild dog sounds kept coming.

Kept coming at him as surely as a laser beam.

As they grew closer, he realized these sounds *weren't* the same. These weren't the annoying, high-pitched little snarly snaps that had greeted him in his nightmares for weeks after that horrifying ambush at Halo Burger. These were much larger dogs. Much more powerful dogs.

Russell picked himself up off the ground and said, "Whew, I sure am glad it's not those doggone Chihuahuas again!"

Just as he said this, an animal appeared.

A dog that was running at full speed, digging its paws into the earth, leaning mightily into the harness that was attached to its powerfully muscular shoulders.

The moment the animal ran into the warmth of the boulevard of Buster B. Bayliss County, it did a quick U-turn and headed back. Back where it belonged. Back to its own world. Back to the world eons of evolution had perfected it for, the world of biting cold and cutting winds.

As that stunning lead animal's tail disappeared into the wall of snow and ice, the head of another magnificent, harnessed dog came out of the cold. It too was running at full tilt. And it too made the U-turn back into its own environment. Six more times another harnessed dog did this. The only sound they were now making was the grunt from the exertion of pulling something heavy, a whoosh that exploded from their open mouths and flaring nostrils.

Finally what they were straining to tow began to emerge from the wall of snow.

A long, low sled made of bent trees and browned strips of leather.

It nearly tipped on its side as it was sharply pulled back to the right, back toward the place in the wall where the team of dogs had disappeared. But it didn't, it stayed upright.

Then Russell saw two of the most amazing things he'd ever seen.

The first was that the sled was being controlled by a most unusual driver.

Russell said, "Now, I've got to think, I can't remember setting any food-eating records here in Ourside, but this sure does look like a twenty-eight-pieces-of-tandoori-chicken-in-fifteen-minutes nightmare."

What was driving the sled was Frosty the Snowman!

A vibrant, alive, six-foot-six-inches-tall and big-around-as-the-moon Frosty.

Just before the sled disappeared back into the wall of snow, Russell saw something very familiar pushing the sled with all its might.

He rubbed his eyes and said, "Rod-Rode?"

Did he actually see his little lost dog? Or *was* this a nightmare?

Frosty jumped off of the sled and hollered, "Pull up, babies!"

The sled stopped so that only the very tips of its rear runners were sticking out of the snow wall, the rest of it invisible in the tempest.

Then the snowman began shuddering, flapping his arms. It seemed he was trying to shake off the snow.

Frosty was becoming smaller and smaller.

And browner and browner.

And furrier and furrier.

A rapidly melting pile of snow gathered at his feet.

Russell said, "Hey, you're not a snowman, you're Smokey the Bear!"

Smokey shook his head from side to side and a pair of ice cubes flew out of his ears.

He said, "What was that you said before? What on earth is 'rat wrote'?"

Russell did the very thing you should do if you ever find yourself in a situation like this: very quietly and very respectfully and very quickly answer Smokey the Bear. (And not just Smokey either, the same would apply to any other bear that happened to ask you something. Worry about if it makes sense later, just make sure you're on your best manners when you answer that bear!)

He said, "No, Mr. Bear, I didn't say 'rat wrote,' I said 'Rod-Rode.' That was my dog Rodney Rodent pushing your sled. I think it was him, it looks like he's grown a lot since the last time I saw him. I don't think it's very nice of you to make him work like that, but I gotta say thank you very much for not eating him."

"Eating him?" the bear nearly roared. "*Eating* him? I'll have you know I'm a vegetarian, young man."

The bear began sputtering, "Besides, what kind of nonsense . . . ," then took his paws and tugged and pulled at his skin until it made a ripping, zipping sound and finally separated. Then it began to fall off of him!

As Russell finally got up enough nerve to raise his eyes and look at the rest of Smokey, he saw it wasn't a bear at all, it *was* a regular man who was wearing a fake-bearskin coat and hood. The man kept on his fake-bearskin mittens.

He roared, "Who in the devil is this Rodney Rodent?"

Russell looked at him. He was a tall guy with a thick, wild black and gray beard and a head full of dreadlocks hanging out from below a Detroit Tigers baseball cap. He was wearing a T-shirt that said "Pink Floyd," a pair of faded blue jeans and brown leather moccasins.

Russell said, "Rodney Rodent is my dog. He's the one who was pushing on the back of your sled. Do you think you could call him back out of that blizzard?"

The man said, "Dog? That was no dog! You think that was a dog?"

The man slapped his head and said, "Now I understand! You're from Earth, from Yourside. Finally! Let me tell you, little fellow, it sure is good to see you!"

The man pulled one fake-bearskin mitten off of his hand, reached out and said, "Bayliss's the name, Buster B. Bayliss. Welcome to my county."

Russell pouted. "Are you *really* Buster B. Bayliss? Really?"

The man pulled a wallet from his back pocket. He said, "Well, if I'm not, I'm in a lot of trouble 'cause I've been carrying his wallet around for years."

Russell shook the author's hand.

"My name's Russell Braithewaite Woods, and no one sent me, sir, I'm here from Flint by mistake."

"Good for you. Now, I hope you're not one of those young people who think every quiet second has to be filled with chatter. Asking millions of questions. Chatter-munks, I call 'em. Can't tolerate 'em. We're here in the North Country to get a job done. Fewer questions you ask, better we'll get along."

Russell pouted again. He was disappointed because he *did* have a million questions to ask Buster B. Bayliss. Questions about writing. Things like, was Ben-Jammin ever going to catch Hair-Man and give him a shave, or would he ever find out who'd put the bald cream in the hair oil bottles, and what was going to happen if Ben-Jammin got attacked by the Ring Worm brothers again, and where did he get his ideas, and what was his favorite color, and what size shoes . . ."

Literary questions.

Buster B. Bayliss put two fingers to his mouth and let a high-pitched, piercing whistle rip. Then he hollered, "Throw it in reverse, Ahjah!"

A shape began to emerge from the wintry barrier.

Rodney Rodent!

But this time Rodney wasn't pushing the sled, he was pulling it! He was standing on his rear legs with his back to Russell and was using his front legs to tug the sled out of the snow! But strangest of all was Rod-Rode's tail, which was digging into the ground and anchoring itself and helping pull the sled backward!

Once the sled appeared, Rodney kept pulling until the hindquarters of a sled dog could be seen. The dog was pulling ferociously in the other direction, trying to run, but Rodney Rodent was moving the sled like the animal wasn't there at all.

Another dog came out of the snowy land, then another, then another, until finally there were eight powerful huskies pulling against Rodney Rodent. Mr. Bayliss whistled again and the dogs collapsed onto their sides, panting so hard you'd've thought they'd just pulled the Rock of Gibraltar to South Africa.

Rodney Rodent let go of the sled, dropped down on all fours, then began chewing at his right front paw.

Buster B. Bayliss roared with laughter. "I love it! It drives those dogs crazy when I have Ahjah pull them in the other direction!"

"Why are you calling Rodney Rodent 'Ahjah'?"

"Oh! That's it! You think Ahjah is your *dog*."

"I know he's my dog, Mr. Bayliss. We got him 'cause we thought Zoopy croaked when he jumped off the dam with Bucko back when we were getting chased by the feds and Agent Fondoo was trying to make it so that we couldn't spend the quadrillion-dollar bill, but all I wanted was a mountain bike, so Mummy and Daddy went to the dog pound and got the littlest dog they could find and I named him Rodney Rodent and he's—"

Buster B. Bayliss held up his hand and said, "Wait! One minute! I hear something!"

He put his hand to his left ear and said, "Yes! I did hear something."

He took the fake-bearskin mitten he'd been wearing and gave Russell a good smack in the back of the head.

Pa-whap!

Buster B. Bayliss said, "I heard the biggest chatter-munk I've ever seen. Must weigh a good two hundred and twenty pounds.

"The fact is Ahjah isn't a dog at all, he's a rare animal called the Madagascar Mountain Munchker. Found only on the eastern slopes of a really big hill in Solon, Ohio.

"Do you honestly think a dog could push or pull like that? Somewhere in their distant past it's believed these animals might have been related to dogs, but now every bit of dogginess has been bred out of them and they have evolved into the purest work animal known in either Ourside or Yourside. They live to push and pull. If they don't get the chance to work, they get smaller and smaller until they finally disappear."

"But he's my *dog*."

"Listen, kid, take my word for it, there's not a single doggy thing left in Ahjah. He's a work animal, pure and simple. Hasn't got the least interest in barking or sniffing or chewing or howling or licking your face or biting your fingers or wagging a tail. . . ."

"But he always used to wag his tail when I'd come home from school."

"Impossible. He doesn't even have a tail."

"Then what's that thingamajiggy sticking out of his booty?"

"It's not a tail, it's actually a prehensile vestige, gives him stability, helps him pull. It may have been a tail way back on his ancestors but not anymore. He grabs the ground with it and tugs."

Every word Buster B. Bayliss said made Russell's frown get bigger and bigger.

Ahjah, or Rodney Rodent, shook his head from side to side and two really small ice cubes flew out of his really small ears.

Russell pouted like a kindergarten baby and said, "Sorry I treated you like you were a dog, Rod-Rode, I guess that's why you wouldn't eat dog food, huh?"

The Madagascar Mountain Munchker's ears perked up when he heard Russell's voice. He turned and looked at Russ and threw his head back and let out a wail just like the one he'd broken Mr. Woods's car window with.

Mr. Bayliss and Russell clapped their hands over their ears. Ahjah's prehensile thingamajiggy began wagging and twirling and spinning so fast and so hard that it turned into something like a helicopter's rotors, and Rodney Rodent lifted right into the air and flew up so that his mouth was next to Russell's face! The diminutive dog began licking Russ's cheek. He looked very much like a hummingbird going at a red flower.

Buster B. Bayliss said, "Well, I'll be a . . ."

Russell couldn't help laughing. He held his hand out and Rodney Rodent gently landed in his palm.

Russell said, "Good boy! Oops! Since Rod-Rode's one of those Munchker things and not a dog, is it okay to say 'good boy' to him, Mr. Bayliss?"

Buster B. Bayliss scratched his beard. "You know what, I've never seen a Madagascar Mountain Munchker act like this. Maybe wee Ahjah here is a hybrid of some kind, maybe he's turning back to some instinctive behavior buried in his genes or maybe . . . maybe he's acting this way 'cause you're an Old . . . n-a-a-h . . . all of the stories say that Old Souls are generally a lot smarter than what you seem to be. This is quite a mystery."

He might as well have been talking to himself. Russell was busy cooing at Rodney Rodent, who was whining right back at him.

Mr. Bayliss said, "Sheesh, what an embarrassment. And to think I thought you might have been one of the Old Souls.

"I hate to have to break up this little lovefest, but we're all here for one reason and one reason alone. We've got to track down and destroy the Ursa Theodora-Saura. If I have anything to say about it, he's terrorized and pillaged his last village here in the North Country."

Russell said, "What's a Ursa Theodora-Saura?"

"It's like the pit bull of bears. A creature so ferocious that even rocks and trees get up and run when it comes near. Hop in the sled, we'll talk about it as we go. All the signs

155

tell me he's trapped in a very small area and after we find out where, it's going to be either him or me, or now that you're here, it's going to be either him or *us*."

"Well, Mr. Bayliss, that's gonna be a problem. . . ." Russell began edging back toward the door that led from Buster B. Bayliss County to Ourside.

"Mummy and Daddy have told me never to take rides from strangers, and even though you *are* my favorite author, you still seem kind of strange."

Russell pointed at his Oops-a-Daisy and said, "Besides, Madam President will kill me if I waste any time in here."

He patted Rodney Rodent on the head and said, "I've already done what I was supposed to do, I rescued my dog, so me and Rod-Rode are gonna have to—"

"Oh, no you don't, buckaroo, I've been chasing that Ursa Theodora-Saura with that team of dogs for six years. Now I'm this close to ending the fear and horror he's caused, and no silly Oops-a-Daisy is going to stop me—stop *us* from completing this mission.

"Nothing is."

Before Russell could think of another excuse, Buster B. Bayliss snatched him by the collar and plopped him into the back of the sled. Ahjah helicoptered himself to the back of the sled, dropped down onto his rear legs and waited for the signal to push.

Mr. Bayliss hollered, "Get-up-uh, get on up!" then whistled. The dogs leapt to their feet and began running, Ahjah started pushing, and it was like a jet's afterburners kicked in as the sled nearly flew back into the land of ice and cold!

Russell shivered and thought, "I sure wish I'd brought Richelle's friend Sweetie, the Great Morose Fire-Spewing Clabbernabber, and some cans of Boston baked beans. This place could really use a couple of good farts to warm it . . . ," but just then the cold hit him hard, and as any of you who have ever been suddenly dumped in the cold know, talking about a gas-passing dragon is about the last thing you want to do when you're worried about being turned into an icicle!

THIRTEEN

Trapped in Buster B. Bayliss County!

THE SLED HADN'T GONE twenty frozen feet when Buster B. Bayliss shouted, "Pull a lefty, my hefties!" and the lead dog veered sharply to the left, heading back into the warm street.

Once the author pulled the sled to a stop, he said, "Look, young man, I've had a change of heart. A brother's got to do what a brother's got to do, and sometimes that involves admitting when you've done something wrong and apologizing. So I'm standing up to my obligation and I'm saying I'm terribly sorry I snatched you into the blizzard the way I just did. That was plain old wrong."

Russell hopped out of the sled and said, "Whew! Thank you, sir, no hard feelings. I'll just take Rodney Rodent and head back to Richie-Rich and Bucko and we can get started on their missions and—"

Buster B. Bayliss said, "Ooh, big misunderstanding. I'm apologizing for snatching you into the blizzard *the way I did*, not for snatching you into the blizzard."

Russell sounded just like someone else we all know when he said, "Huh? I don't get it."

"I'm sorry for snatching you into the blizzard the way I did, *unprepared*. I've searched so long and hard for that wretched Ursa Theodora-Saura that I've got to admit I forgot one of the most important rules for living out here in the wilderness: Always be prepared. I simply forgot your blood isn't used to that snow. So now we'll head back to my summer camp to hunt you up some protective clothing."

Buster B. Bayliss's voice suddenly changed. A sadness was there because he knew the time was very close when he'd have to do something he really didn't want to. Something that went against his very nature. Something he'd been dreading since he'd started hunting the Ursa Theodora-Saura. Something he knew could only end in one tragic way.

He was going to have to kill . . . or be killed.

His eyes looked toward the winter wall and seemed to peer through the snow. He almost whispered, "Yes, we'll get you some clothes."

He sounded even sadder when he said, "And I'll have to bring *it* out."

His dark brown eyes bored even deeper into the snow and crinkled with sorrow. (And if your eyes have ever crinkled, you know how much that hurts!)

He said, "Now *it's* the only thing that can end this reign of terror."

Russell couldn't help himself, a giant GULP! jumped from his throat.

Buster B. Bayliss pulled Russell behind him into the forest.

Deep into the woods.

"Wow!" Russell said. "This is so coo—"

That was all he got out before the North Country mosquitoes discovered him. One second he was breathing in humid, fecund forest air and the next second he was breathing in an army of bloodsuckers.

His nostrils and his mouth and his ears were instantly filled; it was like he was swimming in a lake of them. In two seconds Russell gained eighty-five pounds. Eighty-five pounds of slurping, hungry, winged little devils.

Buster B. Bayliss swung around, and looking through a million mosquito wings, Russell could see he'd lit a small coffee can filled with leaves. The smoke from the burning dried leaves washed over Russ and, just like that, the bugs left him alone.

"Sorry, little buckaroo, I've been over on the cold side for so long it had completely slipped my mind that it was mosquito season over here in the warm side."

Russell blew a long, sticky, wet, squirming tube of mosquitoes out of the left side of his nose, then another one out of the right side. It took him five crunchy chews and two huge swallows to get down the bunch that had flown into his mouth.

Buster B. Bayliss looked at the writhing, wriggling, twisting, jiggling, moist tubes of mosquitoes on the ground and the way Russell was licking his lips, and an expression of disgust washed over his face.

Russell said, "Yum! What time of year is mos-kwee-toe season?"

"Up here it generally runs from about December fifteenth of one year to December fourteenth of the next. But don't worry, once you get some of this smoke on you, they have no interest in biting anymore."

"Hmmm," Russell said, "they taste kind of sweet. Sweet and tangy at the same time. But they could use a little salt."

Mr. Bayliss looked to the sky and muttered, "Please forgive me for thinking this kid was an Old Soul."

Russell said, "Mr. Bayliss, those mos-kwee-toes are real pains when they get in my ears and nose, but is there any way I can get them to fly straight into my mouth?"

Buster B. Bayliss nearly choked. *"What?"*

He took his fake-bearskin mitten and gave Russell a good pop on the back of his head.

"Listen, buckaroo, if you don't quit this chatter-munk chattering and start concentrating on what we've got to do, I'll wear you out with this mitten!"

Russell thought, "Sheesh, for a favorite author he sure is kind of grouchy."

The two walked through the woods in silence. For three hours they trudged down old game trails and along dried riverbeds and through thicket after thicket of forest. While

Buster B. Bayliss's educated eyes saw much, saw the great struggles of nature being played out, saw a multitude of near-invisible hidden animals carefully eyeing them, trying to assess if they were a danger, Russell's eyes saw two things only: Mr. Bayliss's back and the cloud of mosquitoes that still followed them just out of the reach of the smoke.

Russell knew that for some strange reason Mr. B. had been on the verge of throwing up when he saw Russ chew the scrumptious mosquitoes, and it's one of those annoying things about adults that anything you do that makes them gag, they'll force you to stop doing, so he was being very careful not to let the great outdoorsman see that every time Buster B. Bayliss turned his back or disappeared behind a tree for a second, Russell would reach back and grab a handful of the mosquitoes and stuff them into his mouth.

The *real* reason Russell wasn't talking was because he'd been properly raised by his parents and knew it was wrong to speak when his mouth was full. To tell the truth he *was* dying to say something, but the bugs were sooo good!

The main thing Russell wanted to say to Mr. Bayliss was "Are we there yet?"

He began slowing down, and Buster B. Bayliss thought, "I wonder why they'd send a soft little city boy to help me?" But the real reason Russell was lagging was because he'd eaten about thirty pounds of mosquitoes! And how fast do you think *you* could walk behind an author with that many bugs in your belly? Not very.

Much to Russell's relief, Mr. B. finally said, "There she is. There's home. Home."

Buster B. Bayliss's voice echoed what was in his heart. It echoed the thought he couldn't force away. The thought that asked if this would be the last time he'd see this place. If maybe, after the great battle that was soon to happen, he'd never be able to come here again, he'd never be able to *be* again. If he too would finally know what it was like to be on the losing end of the ultimate kill-or-be-killed battle.

Russell looked into the valley.

His breath caught in his throat (or maybe a mosquito got a bite in on the way down; whatever it was, he stopped breathing for a second) when he saw how beautiful the author's home was.

It looked like a wallpaper picture on a computer.

A large log cabin sat in a clearing on a small rise. A pair of snowshoes, a set of antlers and a harness like the one the sled dogs had been attached to hung on the side of the cabin. Underneath the only window on the front of the cabin was an upside-down sled about the same size as the one Rodney Rodent had been pushing.

There was a rocking chair and table next to the front door. Right behind the cabin was another rocking chair and table, a bull's-eye target and a clothesline. About a mile farther back was a 125-foot waterfall! (Nowhere near as impressive as the 250-foot Kearsley Dam waterfall that Steven and Zoopy had jumped off of, but not bad.)

Even from this distance Russell could hear the soothing, soft sound of water churning on rocks.

He said, "Wow! That's so coo—"

Buster B. Bayliss interrupted by almost whispering,

"*Home*. Let's get this started." He began trudging down the path leading to the cabin.

Russell snatched a handful of mosquitoes and followed. He chewed, looked at his Oops-a-Daisy, swallowed and thought, "Man! Madam President is probably real worried about me. But escaping from Buster B. Bayliss and getting Rodney Rodent back shouldn't take more than a couple of hours, I'll be outta here in no time at all!"

If that's what you're counting on, Russell Braithewaite Woods, sorry 'bout your luck!

The only furniture in the cabin was a chair, a table with a big white bowl on it and a large wooden box tucked in one corner.

"Uh-oh, Mr. B., looks like some B-and-E kids cleaned you out!"

"Some who?"

"Breaking-and-entering guys. It looks like they robbed all your stuff."

Buster B. Bayliss looked around the cabin. "Nothing's missing. I talk simple and I live simple. Everything needed is right here."

"Everything?"

"Everything."

"Don't you ever go to the bathroom?"

"*What?*"

"You said you've got everything, but I don't see a bath-room in here."

Buster B. Bayliss shook his head. "Thirty feet behind the cabin, a perfectly good hole."

Russell didn't see what a hole had to do with a bathroom, but there were a lot of other things missing too.

"Where's your bed?"

"I sleep under the stars."

"And your stove and your fridge and your television and your DVD player and your radio and your—"

Buster B. Bayliss put his hand to his ear again and said, "Hold on a minute. . . ."

Russell, being a great detective, knew what was going to happen next, so he was prepared when the fake-bearskin mitten popped the back of his head.

"Oops!" Russell said. "I guess you were hearing a chattermunk, huh?"

"Enough talk. Time to turn in. Up early tomorrow."

Russell said, "Uh, Mr. Bayliss, I hate to burp your bubble but . . ."

He stopped and thought for a second. "Hmmm, if Mr. B. falls asleep, I'll be able to escape! I'll just pretend I'm snoozing, grab Rodney Rodent and leave!"

Russell gave a big fake yawn and said, "Man! I'm really, really sleepy."

He looked at his Oops-a-Daisy and said, "I guess I have plenty of time to—"

Buster B. Bayliss said, "What is that?"

"My Oops-a-Daisy."

"That's what I thought." He put his hand out.

Russell took the Oops-a-Daisy off and handed it to the author.

Buster B. Bayliss put the strange watch in his pocket.

"You'll get it back when we're done. We're running on natural time now. No watches. No clocks. No Oops-a-Daisies."

Russell shrugged. He didn't really understand this thirty days/ninety-nine years stuff anyway. And besides, every time he looked at the Oops-a-Daisy, it just reminded him how much trouble he was going to be in when he saw Madam President.

Buster B. Bayliss said, "There's a hammock out back, string it between two trees and sleep."

Soon Russell was in the hammock, gently swinging between two birch trees. Buster B. Bayliss lit a small fire, threw a sleeping bag on the ground and stretched out on the bag.

"Sleep tight, buckaroo. Tomorrow we search for the first omen."

"What's that?"

"They didn't tell you?"

"Who's they?"

"The people who sent you."

So many people had told Russell so many confusing things since the gnome snatched him that he was having a hard time remembering his own name.

He said, "I guess they did, but I forgot."

"I'll tell you this once. You've been sent to help me stop the Ursa Theodora-Saura."

166

"I think I remember that part but I forgot why we've gotta stop him."

Buster B. Bayliss leaned on his left elbow and stared into the fire.

"We have to stop him because if we don't, he won't be satisfied until he's killed every rabbit in the North Country and nearly every person."

"This thing kills bunnies?"

"Viciously."

"How come you haven't caught him yet, Mr. Bayliss?"

"The North Country is huge."

The author's eyes were drawn up as a shooting star streaked across the sky. He stared at the point where it seemed to disappear and said, "Village after village I've gone to, trying to stop him, but I'm always a day or two late. I'm always left to find the destruction, the carnage."

He tossed a twig into the fire. "There's no way to describe the feeling you get when you come to a village and find every man, woman and child has been torn to shreds.

"Shreds! And this monster isn't killing for food either. He's killing for the sheer joy of destroying. *That's* why we've got to stop him. *That's* why you've been sent here."

Russell thought this was a pretty interesting story, but he was afraid he'd never find out how it ended, because as soon as the great woodsman fell asleep, Russ planned on being outta there!

Buster B. Bayliss said, "The good news is you're here. That means that the battle will be sooner rather than later. One way or the other this nightmare is about to end."

Russell thought, "Nope, what that really means is there's gonna be a very, very surprised person when you wake up tomorrow and find me gone!"

A shooting star caught Russell's attention too. He noticed how much brighter the stars were here and how many more of them there were and how much blacker the sky was. He could hear a stream slapping over rocks not too far away. He heard an owl sadly asking its question and an army of crickets gently chirping. There was something strange about the air too. It seemed like it was slipperier, like it slid deeper into him when he breathed in. And when he breathed out, it felt as if the air leaving his lungs was making him feel lighter and lighter.

"Wow!" Russell groggily thought. "This is so coo . . ."

Russell had been right. There was a *very, very* surprised person at Buster B. Bayliss's cabin early the next morning.

It was a certain future detective from Flint, Michigan.

"All right, buckaroo, up and at 'em."

Russell opened his eyes and blinked.

"Excuse me, sir, there're still stars in the sky and it's still dark."

"Come on. I'm not sure when we'll get the omen that the end's near. You need to learn the woods. Need to learn to look for signs. Need to learn what's important out here."

Russell couldn't believe he'd fallen asleep and blown his chance to get away from his favorite author.

But the sleep he'd had was so relaxing and beautiful that he wanted to know more about life outdoors.

So the lessons began.

And Russell was a great student.

It's true that the sound of a fake-bearskin mitten slapping the back of a head was heard more than once or twice over the next six days, but the young Flintstone learned and grew. And the two became almost friends. Though few words were exchanged between them, they began to understand each other. (Well, I don't think if they spent sixty years together Buster B. Bayliss would understand half of the things that Russell thought about, but Russ understood the author, so that was enough.)

And just six days after he'd planned his escape, a change had taken place in Russell. He was becoming more in tune with nature, he was becoming less of the soft city boy and more of the woodsboy. (And if that's not a word, it should be, along with woodsgirl, woodswoman, woodsbaby, woodscat and woodsdog. I'd draw the line at woodsroach, though.)

Russell was becoming less of a pampered boy from Flint and more of something hard as stone. I guess you could say he was becoming less of a Flintstone and more of a stone flint. I guess you *could* say that, but it would probably be best if you didn't.

But the changes weren't limited to Russell, they also happened to his new friend. A new sense of purpose seemed to come over Buster B. Bayliss, purpose and focus.

Where before he'd been a man of few words, now he was a man of almost no words. Where before he'd been a sort of get-'er-done type of person, he was now a get-'er-done-and-don't-make-a-peep type of guy. Where before he'd been a total loner and completely independent, now he was still those things but he at least was putting up with Russell.

Finally, the day Russell came back to the cabin with a stringer full of fish, Buster B. Bayliss broke the silence. He said, "You're ready."

He grabbed one of the shovels and simply said, "Shovel. Bring."

In his new awareness Russell understood this shortcut way of speaking.

Without a sound he snatched up the other shovel and trudged behind the mountain man. They headed up the steepest hill, and after what seemed to him to be forever Russell finally said something in this new shorthand language.

He said, "There. Yet. We?"

Mr. B. responded, "Mouth. Close. Munk. Chatter."

They walked another half hour before Mr. B. put his hand up, checked his compass and walked north-northwest to a large pine tree. He then headed south-southwest for eight steps, pointed at the ground and said, "Dig."

Russell said, "Whew! Glad. I. Am."

Buster B. Bayliss said, "Enough Cat in the Hat talk, get busy."

The two began flipping shovelfuls of the rich forest floor over their shoulders. Before long Russell's shovel hit something that made a metal-on-metal sound. The scraping sound surprised him but had a much deeper effect on Buster B. Bayliss.

The metallic, hollow sound was proof to him that one of his worst nightmares was about to be revealed. That he was about to unearth something that he'd always hoped would remain buried. Something he'd prayed he'd never have to come back for. But there was no doubt, what was in the metal coffin Russell's shovel had scraped was the only thing that would give him even the hint of a prayer against the Ursa Theodora-Saura.

While Russell had visions of buried treasure dancing around in his head and excitedly worked at unburying the metal box, Buster B. Bayliss, without realizing what he was doing, let his shovel slip from his hands, closed his eyes and drew in three deep breaths.

When his nerves had been steeled, another great change came over him. It was a change brought about by the acceptance that he'd done all he could do, that the years of preparation, both physical and emotional, were finally over and that those years of getting ready for what was about to occur would soon prove to be enough . . . and he'd live, or they would be not enough . . . and he would become one with the forest. He would die.

He knew that one way or the other the end was at hand. And that knowledge brought on a final change. A change that made his back even straighter and his shoulders even broader. A change that brought the great outdoorsman peace.

Steeling your nerves, getting a bunch of knowledge and finding peace takes a lot longer than you might think it would, and by the time Mr. Bayliss finally got to that point, Russell had completely dug out the metal coffin and knocked off the lock. Before he threw the box open, he shouted, "Treasure! Rich! Yahoo!"

Inside there was a jumble of cables and wires, pieces of strangely shaped metal, small wheels, a fancy ink pen, two dimes, a cool sword in a leather sheath, a small leather pouch with a beautiful purple drawstring holding it closed, a little telescope-looking thing, and a locked, long, narrow wooden box that rattled when it was shaken.

Russell looked at Mr. B. and said, "Disappointed. Am. I. No. Bling. Bling."

Buster B. Bayliss might have found peace, but he was still Buster B. Bayliss and Russell had worn out the man's last nerve days ago.

PA-THWOK!

He said, "Look, if you don't cut out that annoying way of talking, I don't know what I'm going to do."

Russell almost said, "Sorry. Am. I," but he had sense enough to put his hand over his mouth and just say, "Oops!"

Without even looking inside, Mr. Bayliss closed the lid and said, "Take one end, I'll take the other. We need to get back to the cabin before nightfall, when the mosquitoes get thick. Then we must prepare for the final chapter. For the end."

Russell wasn't listening too closely to the outdoorsman's words. All he could think was "Nightfall. Skeeters. Yum!"

I hate being a party pooper, but if Russell doesn't start paying closer attention, it's not going to be long before instead of him eating mosquitoes, something's going to be eating him!

FOURTEEN

The Final Omen!

NIGHTFALL WAS STILL a good two hours away when they placed the coffin-shaped box on the table outside the cabin.

Russell was starving! He'd had his hands full the whole way and hadn't been able to eat any mosquitoes.

He ran to the smoked-food box and had eaten two whole pounds of the dried fish before Buster B. Bayliss, sounding an awful lot like a certain former president of the Flint Future Detectives, said, "Huh? I don't get it. Why do you not eat anything for days, then allow yourself to get so hungry you eat like a bear?"

Russell wasn't about to let Mr. B. know that the mosquitoes had been ruining his appetite, so he said, "Mummy says I've got a real strange metal-brawlic rate."

"You've definitely got a real strange *something*, but we

174

haven't got time to figure out what." He paused and added, "We've got to put this together."

The sorrow was back in his voice.

"And I have to practice using it."

The crinkle was back in his eyes.

Yowch!

Mr. B. almost whispered, "I hope I haven't lost the touch."

Both of the woodsguys' eyes were drawn up as a single cloud passed over the sun.

Russell laughed and said, "That cloud looks like Porky Pig eating a bag of pork rinds."

Buster B. Bayliss froze. "*What did you say?*"

Russell pointed. "That one there. It looks like Porky Pig's eating from a bag of pork rinds."

"The Cannibal Cloud of Kenjiro," Mr. Bayliss whispered, "the next-to-last omen of this part of the Chronicles of Zornea-Hu!"

He studied the cloud but couldn't see what Russell had seen. But that wasn't important, Russell had seen it.

Buster B. Bayliss said:

> "*A sign shall come and few will see, within two*
>   *days the fight shall be.*
> *The beast shall shift from cold to hot, and soon*
>   *the Three are in the spot.*
> *The fight's at hand, the tale nearly through, when*
>   *one little piggy on his cousin does chew.*"

Mr. Bayliss stared off into the woods.

Russell gulped and said, "What does that mean?"

"It foretells that the Ursa Theodora-Saura has moved from the cold land into summer land."

He knelt and pulled a piece of grass from the earth.

"Two days."

He tossed the grass back down and stood.

"We'll meet within the next two days."

Another GULP! jumped out of Russ's throat.

Mr. B. carefully took all of the contents out of the coffin and put them on the table.

He separated everything into two piles. In the first pile he put the two dimes, the sword, the small leather bag with the purple drawstring, the long, narrow box and the ink pen. All of the weirdly shaped metal wheels and gadgets and the little telescope thingy were set in the second pile.

He wasted no time in getting to work putting together the equipment from the second pile. What had looked to Russell like a bunch of pulleys and cables and wheels and metal elbows and arms soon turned into a mighty-looking weapon.

A bow.

A bow powerful enough to hurl an arrow into the Man in the Moon's left eye.

Buster B. Bayliss reached into the first pile and picked up the small leather pouch that was held shut by a purple drawstring. He pulled gently on one end of the string and, to Russell's amazement, it turned into a lovely, delicate purple dragonfly! The whole string was a series of dragon-flies holding on to one another's tails!

Mr. B. said, "The Lacy Guardian Flies of Umchumba."

Russell couldn't help wondering if they'd be as tasty as the mosquitoes.

Once they'd flown off, Buster B. Bayliss reached into the leather pouch and removed a long, thin piece of cord. It was bright yellow and seemed to glow with a life of its own.

"The finest hide string ever, wrestled from one of the tentacles of a—"

Russell laughed, slapped his hand over his mouth and said, "You said 'tentacles.' "

Buster B. Bayliss picked up the fake-bearskin mitten and popped the back of Russell's head again.

PA-THWOK!

"Wrestled from one of the *tentacles* of a giant sea squid by the evil Borinquen warrior queen Serrot Ettevizil."

Mr. B. worked for nearly three-quarters of an hour threading the bowstring through the complicated machinery. Sweat dripped from his dreadlocks and eyebrows as he struggled to pull the cord this way, then that.

When he'd finally finished, he extended the bow over his head and said, "It feels the same as it did when I buried it thirty years ago. Now, if only the years have been as kind to my skills and my eye."

He put the bow in his left hand and began to draw the string back with his right.

"Step aside," he said to Russell.

Russell took three giant steps backward. Even though there wasn't an arrow in the bow, he'd learned that when Mr. B. made a suggestion, it was pretty wise to follow it.

Buster B. Bayliss drew the string halfway back and released it.

The thrum sound that came from the bow was as pure as angels singing or, as Steven's dad would say, as beautiful as the Boys Choir of Harlem harmonizing on a Roberta Flack album.

The air immediately around the vibrating string shimmered as if a blast of heat had been produced by Mr. B.'s plucking.

"Wow!" Russell cried. "Now, that's too coo . . ." Then he noticed the look of pain on his new friend's face.

The outdoorsman/author set the bow on the table and looked down at the inside of his left forearm. It was blistered, almost as if it had been burned.

That old sadness crept into his voice when he said, "It still has the power."

Russell pointed at Mr. B.'s arm and said, "Does that happen every time you shoot it?"

Buster B. Bayliss nodded.

"Then why don't you wear something over your arm so you don't get burned?"

"The bowstring is so powerful that it would ignite anything that I used. Only thing it doesn't *completely* incinerate is human flesh. If I were to cover my arm with something, it would only catch afire. Cause much worse burns."

He reached back into the first pile and pulled the long, slender wooden box from it.

He opened the lock, lifted the lid and removed a narrow, midnight blue, velvet-covered package from inside.

He peeled the velvet to the side and revealed three arrows. He gently, almost lovingly, took one of the arrows in his hand.

He stroked the reddish brown wood.

"Wood from the third-highest branch of the second-oldest cedar of Lebanon."

Russell said, "Wow!"

Mr. B. tenderly riffled the feathers at one end of the arrow.

"Feathers plucked from an in-flight, southward-migrating bald eagle that had eaten nothing but northward-migrating chinook salmon."

"Wow!"

He held the arrow's shaft so that the fading sunlight seemed to explode and dance off of the arrowhead. Russell had never seen anything like it. It looked like it was made of liquid mercury, but it held its form like a solid.

"Metal forged from the northwest end of the Lambykins meteorite of 1926."

"Wow!"

A mosquito that had been buzzing the table made the mistake of landing on one edge of the arrowhead. The edge was so sharp that the mosquito's own weight was enough to cause it to be sliced cleanly in two!

The perfectly dissected halves floated gently to the table. Russell's eyes lit up.

He pointed behind Mr. Bayliss, gasped and said, "Is that the Ursa Theodora-Saura?"

Buster B. Bayliss whipped his head around and Russell quickly wet his fingertip, tapped the mosquito halves, then licked them into his mouth.

Mr. B. might have been able to read all the signs of the wilderness, but it seemed he'd forgotten the second-oldest city-boy trick in the world.

Buster B. Bayliss looked back at Russell and said, "No distractions! This must be done. And done the right way."

"Mr. Bayliss, I bet I know where you got these special, magical arrows. I bet you had to trade a wizard some gold coins and a secret map for these arrows. I bet he made you swim through a ocean full of sharks and whales to get them. I bet you had to kill a—"

Buster B. Bayliss said, "Wrong. Got 'em at Kmart. Blue-light special."

He looked to the east, to the setting sun, and said, "Still time to practice. Attack may be as early as sunrise. Come. To the river."

Buster B. Bayliss reached back into the first pile. He put the two dimes in his blue jeans pocket. He handed Russell the ink pen and the box of arrows. He started to hand him the sword but hesitated.

"You've grown a lot in the last week, but please, please, please be careful with this."

He handed Russell the sword. Russell hooked the sheath onto his belt.

The great woodsman and the not-yet-so-great woodsboy walked toward the far end of the river, toward where the waterfalls crashed into a jumble of boulders and rocks. Russell carried the box with the three arrows, and Mr. Bayliss carried the bow and a water pitcher.

Russell had another million questions, but it was nearing sunset and the mosquitoes were starting to get rambunctious again. Before he and Mr. B. had walked twenty feet, he had a serious mouthful of the little critters.

The author set everything down and dug into his left pocket. He pulled one of the dimes out and, reaching his hand toward Russell, said, "For the past week you've been reminding me of a cow chewing cud. Let me have some of that gum you've been chewing, I need to stick this dime on one of those boulders."

Uh-oh!

Russ reached in his mouth and pulled out the lump of half-chewed mosquitoes. He set the damp, wriggling, wetly buzzing wad in Buster B. Bayliss's hand.

Mr. B. looked at it and said, "Disgusting. Absolutely disgusting."

But the mess of skeeters did seem fairly sticky and one of the rules of the woods was to make do with whatever you had, so Mr. B. walked the dime, the pitcher and the bug ball a hundred feet away to one of the boulders near the base of the waterfall.

He reached two feet over his head and stuck the dime to a spot near the top of the boulder. Then he knelt and filled the pitcher with water.

When he'd walked back, he handed Russ the pitcher, picked up the bow and said, "That's approximately how high the Ursa Theodora-Saura's heart is when he's standing on his rear legs. Arrow."

Russell removed one of the mystical arrows.

Mr. B. fit the notch of the arrow into the bowstring.

He raised the bow to shoulder height, drew the string back as far as he could, closed his left eye, looked through the sight, breathed in once, waited between heartbeats and finally released.

THRU-U-U-U-U-M-M-M!

Russell clapped his hands over his ears.

The arrow hissed like a steaming kettle as it flew at the dime, going in a line as straight as a laser beam.

When the arrow and the dime met, there was the briefest ping sound, then a blinding flash of light followed by a tremendous roar.

Both of them grimaced, shut their eyes and turned their heads.

Russell blinked several times, then looked toward the waterfall. He had to blink a few more times to make sure he was seeing what he thought he was seeing.

The boulder was gone!

Where it had once stood there was nothing, not a rock, not a stone, not a pebble.

Russell turned to Mr. B. to say, "Man! That was so coo . . . ," but the woodsman's face was wracked with pain and he was holding his left arm.

Russell understood what the pitcher of water was for. He picked it up and quickly poured the cooling water over the burns on his friend's forearm.

"Thanks, kid."

"No," Russell said, "thank *you*! That was the coolest thing I ever saw! You hit the dime right on that dead president's nose! That was the greatest shot ever! I'm starting to feel sorry for that Ursa monster! He's gonna be toast!"

Through clenched teeth Mr. B. said, "Not going to be that easy. That was a stable target, the bear moves. And while the Ursa Theodora-Saura acts heartless, he does have one. Unfortunately it's the size of a dime. If I don't hit him directly in it, the upper right-hand quadrant of his heart, he'll die slowly, but he'll live long enough to kill me. . . ."

Russell went, GULP! then said, "Whew! It sure is good we've got two arrows left and you'll be able to shoot at him again if you miss."

Buster B. Bayliss looked to the slowly darkening sky.

He said, "I'll get one shot. If I miss . . . I'm dead, buckaroo."

Gulp!

Russell said, "You think if you miss with the second arrow, they'd give me your money back for the third one at Kmart?"

Buster B. Bayliss said, "If I miss, there won't be anyone

to take the arrow back. Once the Ursa is done killing me, he's going to be so upset that he'll kill anything or anyone that he thinks is with me."

Russell went, GULP-GULP!

Mr. B. said, "Besides, there won't be an extra arrow. Two are for practice. One's for the actual attack."

"You mean you've got to shoot another one tonight?"

"Yes, but it's got to be a moving target."

Russell scratched his head and said, "Since you're a vegetarian, I guess that means you can't practice by shooting any animals, huh?"

"Of course I wouldn't. I wouldn't kill anything unless it was my only source of food."

Buster B. Bayliss scratched at his beard and said, "I've still got that one other dime left, but I suppose with you being the pampered little city boy that you are, you wouldn't be too happy about holding it over your head and running with it to let me practice firing at something moving, would you?"

Russell said, "Boy, Mr. Bayliss, Daddy's always saying, 'T'ank goodness the boy's a lot smarter than he looks.' Running with a target over my head is out."

Buster B. Bayliss said, "Then what to do? What to do?"

Russell said, "I've got it! The waterfall! Look at how there are leaves coming over the waterfall. All you have to do is pick one out, aim at it while it's falling and let it rip!"

Mr. B. said, "Kid, your dad's my kind of man. You really *are* a lot smarter than you look!"

He said, "Arrow."

Russell handed him the second arrow. He nocked it into the bow.

"All right, kid, you've got young eyes and can see a lot clearer than I can, but I've got this scope. You describe to me which leaf I'm supposed to shoot, then I'll aim at a dime-sized piece of it as it comes down the falls. Got it?"

"Got it!"

Buster B. Bayliss steeled his nerves, went through his prefiring routine and finally pulled the bowstring back. He nodded at Russell and waited for him to describe the leaf that he would try to pick off.

And he waited.

And he waited.

And he waited even more.

Finally he had to let go of his breath and, huffing and puffing, said to Russell, "What on"—huff-puff—"the dark side"—puff-huff—"of the Ourside moon"—puff-puff-huff-huff—"are you waiting for?"

Russell said, "I was waiting for the right leaf."

"The *what?*"

"You know how clouds have shapes that look like other things? So do leaves, and a couple of those leaves looked like some of my favorite things. Things like puppy dogs, raindrops on roses, whiskers on kittens, so I was waiting for a leaf to come over that had a real mean face on it, that way when you blew it to smithereenos, I wouldn't have nightmares about puppy guts."

Maybe it was the stress of knowing that the ultimate battle was about to take place within the next forty-eight hours. Maybe it was the fact that he'd been searching so intently that he hadn't had a proper night's sleep in months. Maybe it was the knowledge that he would have to kill something if he was going to stop the slaughter in Buster B. Bayliss County, something he felt responsible for creating. Maybe it was simply because Russell could be such an annoying little pain in the . . . but whatever it was, Mr. B. felt something he hadn't felt in years. He felt a strange moisture coming into his eyes and a strange stuffiness coming into his nose.

Once again, sounding very much like a certain soul singer on a certain quadrillion-dollar bill, he said, "Please. Please. Please. I'm begging you. A leaf. Any old stupid leaf."

Russell said, "Oops! Okay. There! The third leaf from the left, the greenish brown one with a big hole in it."

Mr. B.'s woodsman mind instantly registered, "Maple. Chewed on by male caribou. Bad lower left molar."

He sighted, aimed, drew and released.

THRU-U-U-U-M-M-M!

Once again the arrow flew with a flawless trajectory.

Russell saw it make contact dead center with the leaf before the same tremendous flash of light forced him to turn his head and close his eyes.

He knew what was next and had his ears covered by the time the BOOM reached him.

He looked at the waterfall and saw that it had stopped

flowing! A great cloud of steam rose from where the arrow had struck the leaf. Russell said, "Wow! Bull's-eye! You nailed . . ." He turned to look at Mr. B. and fell silent.

Buster B. Bayliss grimaced.

"Is it your arm?"

Smoke oozed from the burns on the woodsman's arm.

Russell poured the rest of the water onto the wounds. But something more seemed to be bothering Mr. B.

"What's wrong? You hit dead center on the leaf, your aim was perfect!"

"No. It hit dead center. I aimed for the lower left corner. We'd be dead by now if I'm that far off tomorrow."

Russell couldn't help thinking this was an exaggeration, or what Great-great-grampa Carter's dictionary would call "hyperbole."

He said, "Well, the good thing is you were real close. But I'm glad you blew *that* leaf up. It looked a lot like that time in gym class when my rotten teacher, Mr. Williams, was throwing dodgeballs at a bunch of us kids and the only place we could hide from him was behind this big poster from the circus."

Mr. Bayliss's entire body stiffened. He grabbed both of Russell's arms and whispered, "What? What did you say it reminded you of?"

Russell said, "It reminded me of that time the only place we could hide from Mr. Williams was behind the circus poster that had the purple elephants on it." He felt a coldness run through Buster B. Bayliss's hands. Then he saw a look on the woodsman's face he'd never seen before and hoped he'd never see again. It was a look very close to fear.

Fear is like a virus. When one person gets it, everyone around them does. Once again Russell fell into an instinctive mode. He instantly called out, "Mummy!"

Buster B. Bayliss said, "The final omen. The final rhyme:

> *"There'll then be a day when an instructor of play*
> *Will search for the way to young children flay.*
> *And though they will squirm and wiggle like*
> *   worms,*
> *He'll hunt them like germs around blue*
> *   pachyderms.*
> *They'll answer the call and one by one fall*
> *And be plastered to walls by brown, rubbery*
> *   balls.*

"It means the tables have been turned."

GULP!

"The Ursa knows."

GULP!

"He knows what I want to do."

GULP!

"He knows I have the bow."

GULP!

"He's no longer the prey."

GULP!

"He's now hunting us."

GULP!

Buster B. Bayliss scanned the east and the west, the north and the south. He took the final arrow and quickly nocked it into the bow.

GULP!

"The attack is moments away!"

Even though Russell's gulper was darn near exhausted (you try gulping seven times in a row. No. Try it. Seriously. See?), it was like it was going to keep gulping until it blew up.

GULP!GULP!GULP!GULP!GULP!GULP!GULP! GULP! . . .

Buster B. Bayliss wet a finger, put it in the wind, then put it to his nose. The look of fear was back. "The cabin," he said. "It's waiting to ambush us near the cabin!"

FIFTEEN

The Horror
or
The Revenge of the Ursa Theodora-Saura

As THE TWO WOODSGUYS began a mad dash back toward the cabin, Russell tried to tell himself that the situation wasn't as dangerous and close to hopeless as Mr. B. was making it seem.

"Mr. Bayliss?"

"What is it?"

"How can you be so sure you have to hit the Ursa Theodora-Saura exactly in one little piece of his heart to kill him? Seems like if that exploding arrow hit anywhere near his heart, he'd be outta here."

Mr. B. stopped running. "You know what? Since those may be real close to the last words you'll ever say, I guess it wouldn't hurt for me to explain something to you."

Russell tried to gulp but apparently his gulper *was*

completely worn out. The only sound he could come up with was half a gulp, GUH . . . !

"Don't forget, buckaroo, we're in Ourside, not back on Earth. And we're in the H.A.L.F. Land district of Ourside, sort of the same way your city of Flint is located in Michigan."

"Okay."

"Not only that, but we're in Buster B. Bayliss County of H.A.L.F. Land."

"Sort of like we're on the north side of Flint."

"No! Nothing like 'we're on the north side of Flint.' Hush and pay attention."

"Oops."

"Remember, the only way anything gets to live in H.A.L.F. Land is if it was a character or a place in one of my books and I never finished writing about it."

"I remember that."

"Which is the reason why I know the only way to kill the Ursa Theodora-Saura. I created him, so I know that the only way to stop him *instantly* is to shoot him right in the upper right quadrant of his heart. Not the lower right quadrant or the upper left one. To stop him from attacking after he's been wounded he must be hit dead in the upper right quadrant of his dime-sized heart."

Russell scratched his head.

"Man, Mr. Bayliss, I'm not trying to be rude, but why in the world would you make a monster so terrible and so hard to stop?"

"Good question. One I've asked myself every night for the past six years. But don't forget, I never did use him in any of my stories, that's why he's here and not living in a book."

"But that doesn't tell why you made him."

"All right, listen. When I was cutting hair, I used to get so upset when some of the brothers would start telling these unrealistic, romantic stories about bears. You know how it goes. They'd talk Winnie the Pooh stuff, Yogi Bear, Smokey the Bear, the Care Bears, the Berenstain Bears, all those cute, cuddly teddy bear things.

"About the only person who ever got it right was this half-bald guy who used to tell about Winnie the Pooh's evil twin brother, the Wool Pooh. Brilliant brother.

"People just don't realize a bear is a dangerous predator. It doesn't see you as much more than a ham sandwich with clothes on. I got so sick of hearing that mess that I wanted to create something to serve as a warning, to let people know that bears aren't cute. That even the ones that are trained are thinking, 'One chance, all I want is one chance to show you this trick that'll make you disappear.' So I wrote about this horrible, nearly indestructible creature. I created this thing that was a giant, bad-attitude bear on steroids. The Ursa Theodora-Saura. And now it's up to me to destroy him . . . or to be destroyed by him."

He paused. "Well, actually I guess it's up to me and *you*."

GUH . . . !

Buster B. Bayliss kept his eyes moving along the woods, his bow at the ready.

"It didn't take long for me to realize I'd gone too far. This creation was simply too terrible. I quickly stopped writing about him, never used him in a book. Didn't know he would come here and cause so much death and destruction. Never realized I was writing about the very thing that may end my life.

"End *our* lives."

GUH . . . !

They silently ran on and finally reached the last hill before the cabin.

Buster B. Bayliss stopped and said, "Since he's hunting us now, he's going to be waiting at the cabin, or he may try to ambush us. This is the perfect place for him to strike. I don't want to scare you, little buckaroo, but the Ursa Theodora-Saura is just over that hill"—he used the ready-to-fire bow to point in the direction of his cabin, then swept the bow all the way around them—"or he's watching us at this very moment. Watching and waiting. Waiting to separate us from our lives. Waiting to make his charge."

Russell studied the look of determination and strength that came over Mr. Bayliss, and for some reason *he* wasn't afraid anymore. It was as if he too realized that nothing could stop what was about to happen. And it brought about a new feeling in Russell's gut. A feeling that made his insides tighten and rumble with strength. A feeling that seemed to sweep over him in waves. He was feeling something new. New and exciting.

It was courage.

Either that or the beginnings of a really bad case of

diarrhea brought on by eating tons of uncooked mosquitoes.

Whatever it was, it took the fear right out of him.

"Mr. Bayliss, I'm ready to do whatever I have to do to
stop this monster from killing any more people and bunnies."

Buster B. Bayliss never took his eyes off the woods
around them. He said, "That's the spirit, buckaroo."

He pointed the bow and arrow back up the hill toward
the cabin. "Climb the hill, see if there's anything fishy
around the cabin. Observe. Notice everything. Look for
even the smallest detail. The slightest change. I'll stay here
in case he's waiting to attack from the rear. Now tell me
what I said so that I can be sure you got it right."

Russell repeated, "Observe. Notice everything. Look for
small details. Look for the slightest change."

He looked Mr. Bayliss in the eye, stood at attention and
saluted him.

Then he bravely turned to walk up the hill. He'd gone
three steps when Buster B. Bayliss said, "Kiddo?"

Russell turned around and saw that Mr. B. was holding
his Russ-whacking mitten.

Uh-oh!

"Yes, Mr. Bayliss?"

"You've grown. I guess we won't be needing this anymore."

He threw the mitten into the woods.

"I'm proud of you, kiddo."

Russell felt a glow in his heart. A spreading warmth. It was the fact that someone he'd admired for years admired him too. It was an acknowledgment of one of the strongest desires in human beings, the desire to be accepted. To be understood. To feel as though you are a part of a family.

It was that or the first twinges of severe heartburn caused by the incredibly filthy habit of eating bloodsucking parasites.

Either way, it made him stand a little taller. It made him a little more determined to get this over with.

He saluted the great outdoorsman again and continued his trek up the hill. To whatever awaited at the cabin. To his destiny.

He repeated, "Observe. Notice everything. Look for slight details. Look for small change."

Russell thought, "Gee, Mr. Bayliss's books must not be selling so hot if he's got me looking around for small change."

When he got near the crest of the hill, he flattened himself to the earth and began crawling the last few feet. He crept toward the large rock that sat right on the top of the hill. Once he was behind it, he'd be able to see clearly into the valley and Buster B. Bayliss's cabin.

When he reached the rock, he paused. He rolled over, flat on his back, trying to catch his breath. He didn't realize how hard he'd been breathing. He hadn't noticed how tiring the run up the hill had been. How much stress he was under.

After two or three minutes he'd calmed himself. He leaned on his elbows and peeked around the rock to see if there were any differences around the cabin. Anything that might give him a clue that the Ursa Theodora-Saura had been there. Russell was observing. Noticing the slightest detail.

His eyes quickly scanned the valley, then settled on the cabin.

Nothing unusual.

The table, right where it belonged.

A ribbon of smoke rising from the chimney, like always.

Mr. B.'s whittling chair still sat near the cabin's front door. Right next to the humungous, twenty-five-foot-tall stuffed teddy bear someone had leaned against the cabin while they'd been out in the woods.

Nothing unusual.

His eyes swept behind the cabin.

Nothing unusual.

The clothesline, still strung from the cabin to the big tree. Still hung with thirty feet of Buster Bayliss's drying clothes. Just as it had always been.

Nothing unusual.

Russell's hammock, still swinging lazily between the trees. Right next to the twenty-foot-tall grazing moose that had a rack of antlers wider than the entire cabin.

Nothing unusual.

Russell began to slide back down the hill to tell Mr. Bayliss the coast was clear when something a *little* unusual did happen.

The huge moose began walking toward the front of the cabin, then froze in midstride. It noticed the teddy bear. It raised its head high, then snorted and bellowed loudly twice. The sound reverberated throughout the valley.

Startled birds in the woods threw themselves skyward.

The moose dropped its head and, never taking its eyes off the teddy bear, viciously slammed its front paw into the ground seven or eight times.

Not only could Russell see and hear the power of each blow, he could also feel the ground beneath him tremble. From a hundred feet away.

"Wow!" Russell thought. "Now that's coo . . ."

Then something *really* unusual happened.

And Russell froze in midsentence.

The giant, brown, cuddly-looking teddy bear turned his head and peered in the direction of the furious moose!

A stuffed teddy bear turned his head!

The teddy bear staggered onto his cute, chubby back legs. His head towered ten feet over the cabin!

"Oh, man!" Russell thought. "What a great toy teddy bear! It must have a remote control somewhere to make it move!"

The moose pawed the ground four more times.

Russell knew exactly what was about to happen and couldn't bear to watch.

He barreled down the hillside toward where Mr. B. was.

"Mr. Bayliss! It's horrible! You've got to stop it!"

Buster B. Bayliss kept the bow raised toward the crest of

the hill, waiting for any kind of movement. He said, "You saw him? You saw the Ursa Theodora-Saura?"

Russell looked in his friend's eyes and shook his head. "No!" he said. "This gigantic, horrible, mean moose is about to rip a real big, cute, cuddly stuffed teddy bear to shreds! Hurry up and come shoot him!"

Buster B. Bayliss's face changed, and for a second Russell thought he saw the woodsman's hand tremble a bit on the bow.

Mr. B. blinked the sweat from his eyes, swallowed once, then whispered, "So this is how it ends, not with a bang, but with a . . ."

He never finished his sentence.

The drumming sound of enormous hooves pounding into the ground could be heard from the other side of the hill. From the area of the cabin.

Russell thought, "We're too late, the moose is charging! He's going to ruin that cool toy!"

Exactly fifteen times the hooves dug into the dirt. Fifteen steps for the moose to cover the ground between itself and the teddy bear.

Fifteen drumbeats before the most horrible, pain-filled scream either of them had ever heard pierced both of their souls.

Trees seemed to sway.

Rocks seemed to tremble.

Then it ended.

But the echo of pain rolled across the valley.

And it changed every living thing that heard it.

Mr. Bayliss scrambled up the hill. The woodsman positioned himself behind the rock.

In no time at all Russell was standing beside him.

Buster B. Bayliss peeked from one side of the boulder and Russell Woods peeked from the other.

The moose had missed! It must've been bluffing, it must've just run off into the woods! The toy teddy was all right! The only thing that looked different was that now the bear looked like he was wearing some kind of great big hat!

Then the teddy bear let out four of the most disgusting belches Russell had ever heard!

"Man," Russell thought, "whatever toy company made this teddy bear sure didn't give him any kind of manners."

And to make matters worse, after each of the four belches the teddy bear spit out something that was three feet across and shaped like a giant hockey puck!

Russell looked to Mr. Bayliss for an explanation.

"Moose hooves. The filthy thing ate the moose whole. Then made a hat out of his antlers."

"You mean *that's* the . . ."

"Russell Woods, meet the dreaded Ursa Theodora-Saura!"

The monster stood on his rear legs again. His adorable little button nose sniffed the air. He'd caught the smell of the two hunters, but he couldn't pinpoint where the scent was coming from.

In his frustration he roared, and every hair on both Russell's and Buster B. Bayliss's heads stood straight up! (And if you've ever seen a set of dreadlocks stand straight up, you know you've seen something pretty special!) In fact, a quarter-sized patch of hair in the front of Russell's head turned snowy white!

And two of the gray dreadlocks on the front of Mr. Bayliss's head turned jet black!

An army of terrified, panicked rabbits appeared from nowhere and just as quickly disappeared.

The Ursa Theodora-Saura swung one of his front legs at the cabin.

The cabin exploded!

Logs that were two feet thick flew high into the air and came back to Earth as a shower of toothpicks.

The cabin had completely disappeared!

That was good enough for Russell! He started scooching down the hill and whispered back, "Uh, Mr. Bayliss, maybe this hunting the Ursa thingy isn't such a good idea after all. Maybe we should come back when we've got some better weapons, maybe it would be a fair fight if we got a tank and a bazooka and a Humvee and a . . ."

But Buster B. Bayliss knew this was the time. Knew the monster was growing stronger and wiser every day and that he had to be stopped here. He knew that within the next few minutes they'd be victorious . . . or they'd be teddy bear chow.

He stepped from behind the boulder. He raised the bow

and shouted, "HERE WE ARE, YOU MANGY DEATH MACHINE! HERE WE ARE, YOU COWARDLY DE-STROYER OF WORLDS!"

"Oh, man," Russell thought, "why did Mr. Bayliss choose now to quit being the strong, silent type?"

"H-E-E-E-ERE!"

The Ursa Theodora-Saura dropped to all fours and turned in the direction of his next victim's voice.

Russell didn't know why, maybe it was because he wanted to be next to Mr. B. at the end, maybe it was because he didn't want to die alone, maybe it was a change in him as small as .01%, but he scrambled back up the hill and stood shoulder to shoulder with his favorite author.

Buster B. Bayliss shouted, "Supper's on, you odorous fur ball!"

Russell said, "In Flint if we wanna get someone really mad, we talk about their mother. Try telling him his mummy looks like Boo Boo Bear."

What Russell saw next was enough to get his gulper working again!

GULP!

The Ursa Theodora-Saura's adorable little eyes suddenly turned vicious and locked in on the fools on the hill.

GULP!

He pulled himself to his full twenty-five-foot height, and for the first time Russell saw his mouth. He'd never again use *cute* or *cuddly* or *adorable* or *chubby little* to describe this beast.

One word came to mind as he looked down the throat of the superpredator.

Death.

Vicious, agonizing, bone-and-flesh-grinding death.

The monster roared, then began to charge, covering huge expanses of land with each bound.

Whoever said that trees and rocks ran in terror whenever the Ursa Theodora-Saura began to charge had been exaggerating.

But just a little.

Actually only small stones and young saplings came to life and fled in panic.

Russell stepped to the side so that Mr. Bayliss could get a clean shot.

When the charging beast was fifty yards off, Russell noticed how Mr. B. drew the bowstring back as far as it would go, sighted carefully, held his breath, waited between heartbeats and finally . . .

Just as he released the arrow, one of the terrified saplings flew up the hill and brushed Buster B. Bayliss's arm.

THRU-U-U-U-M-M-M!

Buster B. Bayliss screamed, "NO-O-O-O!"

The arrow *was* headed directly toward the Ursa Theodora-Saura, but had the sapling affected Mr. B.'s aim?

This arrow was traveling much faster than the others that Mr. B. had fired.

Russell saw the arrow for only a split second before he put his fingers over his eyes to protect them from the brilliant flash of light he knew would come. He jammed his thumbs in his ears for the inevitable explosion.

The flash of light hit them; then the boom washed over them.

When Russell opened his eyes, a cloud of smoke covered everything near where the Ursa Theodora-Saura had been.

Once again Buster B. Bayliss said, but softly this time, "No!"

Russell looked to where the smoke had blown away.

Where the Ursa had been there was nothing but a large, smoldering pit.

Russell's heart soared!

"We got him! We . . ."

The sadness was back in Buster B. Bayliss's voice, but this time it seemed deeper, it seemed more complete.

He said, "Well, buckaroo, we gave it our best shot. Hand me the last two things that were in the coffin."

Russell smiled, reached in his pocket and handed Buster B. Bayliss the pen, then unhooked the sword from his belt. He figured the sword would be used in a victory salute and that Mr. B. would write something about their win over the Ursa Theodora-Saura with the pen. But Mr. Bayliss gave him the sword back and smiled lovingly at the pen.

"What's wrong? That was a great shot! The Ursa Theodora-Saura is gone!"

Buster B. Bayliss said, "A good hunter knows as soon as

he releases the arrow. I know. Wasn't even close. Hit six and a half inches in front of it. Didn't even wound him."

Russell pointed toward the cabin. "Look, Mr. Bayliss, he's disappeared, there's nothing there but a hole!

"That was so coo . . ."

Then Russell saw it.

Saw an enormous paw reach out of the pit. Then saw a set of huge moose antlers. Then a whole head. Then saw twenty-five feet of teddy bear pull himself out until he stood, obviously dazed.

The Ursa Theodora-Saura shook his head for several seconds, then stared in the direction of the hill. Trying to find his next meal. Trying to find his tormentors.

Russell looked at Mr. Bayliss.

The woodsman had changed.

The author was at peace.

Even though his left forearm was smoking and blistered and smoldering like a Christmas log, Russell could see he was at peace.

He looked at Russell and smiled. "Sorry I got you involved in this, kiddo. Hoped it would have ended differently. All we've got now is one shot, if you want to call it that. I'm afraid there's only about a one-in-a-quadrillion chance that it'll work."

In Russell's mind this was great news! In every book he'd ever read and in every movie he'd ever seen whenever there was a one-in-ten-trillion chance or a one-in-fifty-six-billion chance or even a one-in-a-quadrillion chance of something happening, *it always happened! Every single time!*

But when he saw what Mr. Bayliss called their last chance, Russell started thinking that maybe, just maybe, movies and books weren't always telling the truth.

Buster B. Bayliss walked about five feet down the back side of the hill, away from the still-dazed Ursa Theodora-Saura. He stopped and said to Russell, "There's no point in running. Just drags out what's gonna happen. If I fail, I want you to take the sword, go to the base of the hill and do exactly what I'm going to do. It's not much of a chance. But it's your only one."

Buster B. Bayliss looked back up toward the top of the hill, kissed the pen, and then, stiffening his arm as much as he could, extended the pen toward the top of the hill.

Russell said, "What are you doing, Mr. B.?"

"When he comes barreling over the hill, he'll see me and charge. I'm hoping in his rage he'll come directly at me and try to swallow me whole. If he does, maybe I'll be able to hit his heart with the pen."

This didn't sound like such a hot plan to Russell.

"Wouldn't you have better luck with the sword?"

Buster B. Bayliss laughed heartily and said, "I was hoping you'd ask that, buckaroo. Now I get to tell you, as everyone knows, *the pen is mightier than the sword!*"

"But Mr. Bayliss, as big as that thing is, if he's close enough for you to stab, he'll crush you even if he does die right away."

Buster B. Bayliss said, "I'm a goner, kiddo. But maybe my last act will save you. Maybe I can pull some good out of this."

205

Russ said, "Wait a minute, since this is H.A.L.F. Land, doesn't that mean that you won't really die? Doesn't that mean that back on Earth, on Yourside, you'll still be alive?"

"No. What happens here is real. I'll die here and disappear from Earth. Never to be seen again. Gone."

"But . . ."

"Time to go, kiddo. If you do make it back, tell 'em not to mourn too much for me. Tell 'em I had a great life. Saw things most can only dream about. Went places most don't even know exist. Tell 'em I had the greatest luck, did something for a living that I loved. I actually wrote books. Made whole bunches of kids smile and go 'Oooh!' or 'Wow!' or 'I can do that too!'

"Doesn't get much better than that.

"Tell 'em not to cry for me, tell 'em just to look at the northern lights and know that Buster B. Bayliss is admiring 'em too, only from another place. From another side.

"Now, get on down to the foot of the hill and keep your fingers crossed that there's one more bit of magic that I can do with an ink pen."

Russell didn't want Buster B. Bayliss to see the tears in his eyes, so he did what he was told.

Another deafening roar rolled over from the other side of the hill, followed by the sound of gigantic teddy bear feet charging.

A blizzard of tiny, terrorized stones and an ocean of frightened saplings poured over the hill. Trying to escape.

Russell could hear trees being snapped in half by the oncoming monster.

Then a set of antlers as wide as a charging African elephant's ears appeared at the crest of the hill.

Everything seemed to start moving in super slow motion.

And as the horrible mouth of the Ursa Theodora-Saura finally appeared at the top of the hill, Russell Braithewaite Woods was still learning. And Buster B. Bayliss was still teaching. He taught something about courage. About what true bravery was.

Even with the monster's head so close that they could see ragged patches of moose fur and hundreds of chewed-up rabbit tails and blood dripping from his mouth, even though they were so near that a smell so putrid that it seemed to have color poured from these jaws of death and rolled over them, even though they were so close that the final roar of the Ursa Theodora-Saura blew Buster B. Bayliss's Detroit Tigers cap off, Russell couldn't help feeling impressed.

His favorite author never even flinched.

Russell extended the sword up the hill.

And awaited his turn.

SIXTEEN

Some Pretty Good Proof That Rhythm and Blues Just Might Be the Greatest Music Ever

THE URSA THEODORA-SAURA paused when his entire body was atop the hill. He knew he had time on his side. He knew better than to rush in.

Buster B. Bayliss hollered to Russell, "Just what I was afraid of. He *is* getting smarter. He'll bring death coolly."

Russell said, "But Mr. Bayliss, he doesn't seem real smart to me. You've only got a pen, and I don't want to be the one to burp your bubble, but even a city boy like me sees this isn't going to be much of a battle. Bucko's great-great-granddaddy's mean old dictionary would say this is gonna be a rout."

Mr. B. raised the pen over his head, preparing to bring it down in a stabbing motion, and said, "Oh, no, Russell, this thing is smart, he can't afford to be injured in any way, he needs to be healthy to hunt. The Ursa Theodora-Saura has never faced anything like me, so he's going to take his time and make sure I can't hurt him.

"The good news is this is going to be over quickly. The bad news is our odds of surviving just dropped to one in *five* quadrillion."

The Ursa fell to all fours.

Russell said, "Mr. B., I was thinking, you created that thing, and that's the only reason he's here in H.A.L.F. Land, right?"

Buster B. Bayliss kept his eyes on the monster.

"Correct."

"Then doesn't that mean he has to follow all of the rules here?"

The Ursa Theodora-Saura reared onto his back legs, showing his terrifying twenty-five-foot height.

"Right, he has to follow all of the rules."

"Then doesn't that mean if you'd ever written an ending to his story, he would have to leave?"

The Ursa leaned down and threw another tremendous roar inches from Buster B. Bayliss's nose. The author's dreads flew back and bear slob splashed on his face and dripped off of his eyebrows and chin like he'd been caught in a hurricane. Another couple of his gray dreads turned black.

But he never flinched.

He said, "Oh, that stinks! Worse case of funk-a-tosis I've ever smelled."

Russell yelled, "Wouldn't the Ursa thingy have to disappear if you finished writing about him?"

Mr. Bayliss looked surprised. "You know what, kiddo? That's the first thing I should've thought of. Never occurred to me. My goodness, the prophecy was right, you *did* have the answer."

The Ursa violently swung his left paw at Mr. B. He seemed to have sensed that the only threat to him, regardless of how tiny, was the ink pen. Its aim was perfectly accurate. The pen flew like an arrow for forty feet, then with a resounding THUNK, lodged in an old oak tree.

The beast was toying with his creator.

Russell's hands covered his ears as the Ursa roared again. And it wasn't a roar like you'd hear on television or in the movies either, it was a roar that reached all the way down into both of the outdoorsguys' cells, all the way into their hearts.

Buster B. Bayliss said, "You really had the answer all along."

Russell's voice cracked with fear and sorrow. "Yeah, I had the answer, but I didn't think of it in time."

Mr. Bayliss said, "Well, technically you did. One of the rules for authors who are sent here is that if we ever want to return to the door to Ourside, all we have to do is recite a line from a certain old R & B song."

The Ursa Theodora-Saura had decided how he was going to kill his creator.

Slowly.

Painfully.

He waddled up until he was so close that Mr. Bayliss began throwing punches into his cottony-soft, cuddly underbelly.

Russell screamed, "He's going to try to crush you! Say the words!"

Buster B. Bayliss threw a right and a left, an uppercut and a cross.

The Ursa began to shift his weight backward, preparing to bring all 3,541 of his pounds down on Mr. B.

Buster B. Bayliss kept swinging and said, "Bad news, Buckaroo!"

Right cross.

"Can't remember what the words are."

Left hook.

"Kind of wish I had different musical tastes. Don't know if you noticed the Pink Floyd T-shirt. Folks used to tell me I'd pay a price for being a brother who liked rock and roll. But oh well."

Left jab.

"Never could see the sense in being a fan of a group called the Funky Smellics."

Right, left, right.

Russell screamed, "Funkadelic! Not the Funky Smellics! And I know the song!"

Russell charged up the hill, tackled Buster B. Bayliss around the waist and hollered out, "Bow-wow-wow-yippee-yo-yippee-yay!"

The Ursa's front paws landed firmly on Buster B. Bayliss's head. With Russell's arms wrapped around the woodsman's waist it looked like both of them were going to be driven twenty feet into the ground!

The next thing Russell knew, he and the author were tumbling to the ground back on the grass-covered street between the winter world and the thick forest.

Buster B. Bayliss said, "Thanks a million, kiddo! It's funny, just as he attacked, I decided I really wasn't quite ready to see what the other side of the northern lights looks like!"

Rodney Rodent helicoptered over to where the two were sprawled on the ground and began licking Russell's face.

"Rodney! Man, am I glad to see you! You aren't gonna believe it when I tell you what happened!"

Buster B. Bayliss yelled, "Face time, my poochies," and his sled dogs appeared out of the wall of snow. He rummaged around in the back of the sled, pulled out a laptop computer and squatted.

Russell had never seen a pair of hands move so quickly on a computer. Fifteen minutes after he began typing, the keys of Buster B. Bayliss's computer got so hot they burst into flames. He quickly pulled a disc out of the drive and said, "Darn keyboards last a lot longer in the cold."

Russell said, "What did you do? Did you finish the story about the Ursa?"

Buster B. Bayliss said, "Better than finish it. Did

something else. If you can hold your team, buckaroo, in about five seconds you'll see how I corrected my mistake with the dreaded Ursa Theodora-Saura."

Russell jumped to his feet and stared at the forest wall. The sound that was coming from between the trees terrified him! Even though it sounded like it was coming from ten miles away, there was no doubt that it was the Ursa Theodora-Saura! And man, did he sound mad!

Russell quickly shot a look at Mr. B. and realized that the author had lost his mind. He was laughing insanely! Coming so close to death had done something terrible to Russell's favorite author.

Russ said, "Mr. Bayliss! You were supposed to finish the story! That's the only way the Ursa would disappear! Now the computer is ruined and you can't do any more writing! I don't wanna see that thing again!"

Russell ran toward the door to Ourside.

Buster B. Bayliss kept laughing and said, "Hold on, buckaroo. The Ursa has gotten so smart that he's figured out the rules and knows where we are. He should be here any second now."

Russell couldn't remember if he should turn the doorknob three and a half times to the right or to the left. He fumbled at the knob.

Before Russell could wiggle the knob, the Ursa Theodora-Saura burst out of the woods with a vicious roar.

He had come to finish the job. To finish the lives of Buster B. Bayliss, author, and Russell Woods, future detective.

Some very strange things started happening. And those of you who know about strange things remember they always happen in threes.

The first strange thing was Buster B. Bayliss laughed so hard that even his sled dogs were giving him worried looks.

The second strange thing was that even though he was only ten feet from them, it *still* sounded like the Ursa was ten miles away!

The third strange thing was that the Ursa Theodora-Saura was now about the size of a hamster!

And if you were ever to see something the size of a hamster standing on its rear legs, roaring to intimidate and frighten someone, you'd do the same thing Russell and Mr. Bayliss and Rodney Rodent did; you'd just about bust a gut too!

The hamster Ursa thingy dropped to all fours and charged at Buster B. Bayliss. The only thing he could do was chew on the brown fringe of Mr. B.'s left moccasin.

Grabbing him by the scruff of his neck, Buster B. Bayliss brought the tiny teddy bear up to his face. "I'd say you're in need of an attitude adjustment, little fella."

Russell felt a chill run down his back. The way the Ursa hamster was snarling and snapping and yipping and yapping reminded him of a certain group of small Mexican dogs, an unfortunate meeting at Halo Burger and a couple of stolen fish sandwiches.

His heart skipped a beat when he noticed a flurry of movement coming from the floor of the forest side of the boulevard.

Had the Chihuahuas found him again?

Russell whipped his head around and said, "Whew!"

There were no Chihuahuas, but there was a gathering bunch of rabbits staring at the cute little Ursa hamster dangling from Buster B. Bayliss's hand. And it was obvious from the expression on their faces that they had something no-good in mind!

Buster B. Bayliss saw the disgruntled bunnies, turned to the dangling Ursa hamster and said, "Uh-oh! I think these rabbits might have some questions about your eating habits they'd like to discuss."

The group of rabbits was growing larger and larger and making a very unbunnylike grumbling, growling sound.

Buster B. Bayliss set the Ursa hamster on the ground. He did a cartoon double take at the river of growling, charging rabbits and tore into the land of ice and snow, running with his tail between his legs and yipping like he was on fire.

It took five minutes for the parade of vengeful rabbits to pass.

When the last little cottontail had disappeared into the land of ice and snow, Buster B. Bayliss gave Russell a certain look and said, "Well, buckaroo, I guess all of the prophecies for my county have been fulfilled. Looks like you might be one of the Old Souls after all."

He offered his right hand.

"You've done a lot of growing in the short time we were together. You've learned a lot. A lot about the woods. About living. Not sure how much is going to stick. The longer you're away from the forest, the more of your learning you'll lose."

He put his left fist over his mouth and cleared his throat.

"You know. Never thought I'd say something like this. Been pretty much a loner all my life."

The great outdoorsman cleared his throat again.

"But if you'd like to stay here, I'd . . . er-erm . . . be proud to have you as a . . . uh . . . as a sidekick."

Buster B. Bayliss gave Russell a certain look.

A look that he usually reserved only for the animals in the woods.

The animals he understood.

The animals he felt one with.

The animals he loved.

It was a look of well-earned respect.

It was either that or the beginnings of constipation, for Mr. B. had also discovered the delightfully robust and tangy flavor of fresh mosquitoes and, when Russell wasn't looking, had been himself scarfing down mouthfuls for the past three days.

Whatever this look was, Russell wanted no part of it.

"Thank you, Mr. Bayliss, but I've gotta find Bucko and Richelle and we have to get back to Flint before the Oops-a-Daisy goes off. But if we don't make it, I'll come back and see you."

Buster B. Bayliss had been right, for Russell was already losing his knowledge of the woods.

His need to be super attentive.

His ability to notice every little thing.

Because he didn't even notice that the final time Buster B. Bayliss seemed to choke up and put his hand over his mouth and clear his throat, it was actually a burp, and three terrified mosquitoes fled from his mouth and headed back to the forest, full of tales of imprisonment and terror.

Russell was suddenly very nervous. He swallowed twice, looked at his little dog and said, "Rod-Rode, or Ahjah, whoever you are today, are you staying here or are you coming home?"

The little Madagascar Mountain Munchker looked at Buster B. Bayliss, then at Russell. Three times his head turned from one to the other.

Finally he helicoptered over to Mr. B.

Russell's heart sank and his mouth turned into a giant lowercase letter *n*. He knew whatever Rodney Rodent chose was the best for him.

That didn't make saying goodbye any easier, though.

Rodney Rodent gave the outdoorsman's cheek a quick lick, then hovered over to Russell's shoulder, where he landed and sat down.

Russell quickly shook Buster B. Bayliss's hand, got his Oops-a-Daisy back, gently set Rodney Rodent in his shirt pocket and opened the door to Ourside.

He might have started forgetting all he'd learned about the woods, but it seemed like he had learned one new thing. All at once the whining that Rodney Rodent was doing started making sense!

He was talking!

And Russell understood everything!

He looked down into his pocket and was shocked to hear his little dog say, "Big buddy! I'm telling you the truth right now, I'd never lie to you. I loved my job in Bayliss Land, I love to work, it's true. But olive burgs and weather-balls have been a giant hint. I'm a Flintstone to the bone, big bud, let's bounce on back to Flint!"

SEVENTEEN
Of Munchkers and Men . . .

The door from Buster B. Bayliss County shut behind Russell. Marvin Surly-Guide smiled and snarled, "Aha! What did I tell you? Exactly one week. And thank goodness the goof got away from that monster! Now I'll have a clean record."

Russell didn't need Great-great-grampa Carter's dictionary to tell him what the look on Richelle's face was. Once again it was mortification.

She said, "Russell! How could you run off like that? That was so irresponsible! We've been waiting here a whole week!"

She put her Oops-a-Daisy one inch from Russell's nose and said, "Now we only have twenty-two days, twenty-three hours, nineteen minutes and fifty-two seconds before ninety-nine years go by in Flint! What were you thinking?"

Marvin said, "Hmmm? What was he thinking? Seems to me like the talking book made a mistake when it said you were the smartest in this little gang. Seems to me *any* kind of idiot would know that neither one of your traveling buddies is real big on thinking at all."

Richelle snapped, "Listen, I've had just about enough of you! If you can't say or contribute something positive, just keep your mouth shut!"

Surly-Guide said, "Oooh! I guess you told me, didn't you?"

Russell said, "I'm real sorry, Madam President, but don't worry, I already got punished real bad for what I did. Buster B. Bayliss made sure I got dramatized every single day for a whole week."

Russell raised his right hand. "But cross my heart, hope to die, stick a hundred needles in my eye if I'll ever run off without asking again."

Richelle said, "I hope so, Russell. We were worried sick."

She touched Russell's head and said, "Why is your hair white in this spot?"

She gave Russell a big hug.

He made a face like he'd been bitten by a rattlesnake. "Oh, yuck, Madam President! Stop looking at me! You got the same disease as Bucko, except you think *I'm* the one who's so hot."

Richelle twisted her lips to the right and said, "Dream on, Russell, that was only because it's such a relief to see you."

Steven said, "Heya, Russ," and acted like he was going to hug him too but stopped.

Russell said, "Heya, Bucko," and acted like he was going to hug Steven but didn't.

Richelle said, "Boys! Yuck!"

Russell said, "Whew, Bucko! I'm glad *you* didn't hug me, for a second I thought you fell in love with me too."

Steven said, "Uh-uh! I'm cured. I haven't looked at Richelle in a week, and now I bet I can look at her and see her for what she really is. . . ."

He looked at Richelle. "Yup, I can see she's . . . she's still . . ." He couldn't help himself, he began singing in a real deep voice, "Dark and lovely, you over there, new age lady, independent girl, you're very special and you're so unique. . . ."

Marvin, Russell, Richelle and even Steven himself yelled, "LOOK AWAY!"

Richelle said, "We are so far behind! We've lost a week and haven't even found a clue as to where Rodney Rodent is yet! If we don't stick together, we'll never be able to—"

Russell reached in his shirt pocket and pulled out the shiveringest, shakingest, quivering-quakingest dog anyone had ever seen.

Richelle and Steven yelled, "Rodney Rodent!"

Surly-Guide said, "Oh, joy. One of those filthy Madagascar Mountain Munchkers."

Rodney Rodent looked in the direction of Surly-Guide and whined, but only Russell understood he was saying,

"Big buddy! I can't believe you know this guy, I can't believe he's here. I know you're smarter than your friends, so please lend me your ear. Everyone knows throughout Ourside this is one tricky young man. Make sure you keep both eyes on him and lose him when you can!"

Russell said, "Okay, Rod-Rode, I understand."

Steven said, "You understand what, Russell?"

"Uh, nothing. I was just acting a little dramatized but I'm feeling much better now."

Richelle petted Rodney Rodent and said, "Great work, Russell! Now let's get back to Mr. Chickee and Ms. Tiptip. We don't have any idea how long the second messy mission Mr. Chickee's going to send us on will take, but if we average a week to ten days on each one, it's going to be too close. Are you ready, Surly-Guide?"

The guide grumbled, "Am I ready to get rid of you three pains? I was ready a week ago and I'm even readier now."

Richelle growled, "You're not half as ready to get rid of us as we are to get rid of you! All you need to do is zip your lip and take us back to where we came in."

"Fine. But there is the little matter of payment that we need to take care of first. I believe it was mentioned that if I got you back safely, you'd give me your cool talking book." He grabbed at the thumb drive dangling from Steven's neck.

Steven wrapped his hand around Great-great-grampa Carter's dictionary and said, "Maybe it was mentioned, but not by us, it was by you. Ms. Tiptip already told us what we're supposed to pay you and we'll take care of that when you get us back."

Marvin smiled greasily. "Oh-ho! You guys aren't as un-slick as you look! All right, let's get going."

He pointed at the dictionary and said, "But I'm telling you now, it's meant to be that that talking book is mine."

Rodney Rodent whined, "Big buddy, I hope you listen to me, I hope you mind my word. This surly teenage guiding kid is a low-down dirty bird. He'll steal that talking book, he'll get it from Buck-oh. He'll disappear and won't come back, these are things you should know."

Russell said, "Got ya, Rod-Rode, I'll tell Bucko."

Marvin said, "Would you shut that Munchker up? All that whining gets on my nerves. Come on, I know a short-cut back to Mr. Chickee's crib."

After a much shorter walk the guide opened a door on a porch and the Flint Future Detectives found themselves back in front of Mr. Chickee's house.

"Whew!" Russell said.

Marvin Surly-Guide said, "Okay, you're back safe. Mission completed. The talking book, hand it over."

Steven said, "I'm *not* giving you the dictionary, my dad would kill me if I lost it. Follow us into Mr. Chickee's and we'll pay you the regular guide fee."

The guide said, "Plus I believe I deserve the customary Ourside twenty-five-percent tip."

Great-great-grampa Carter's dictionary said, "Here are the only two tips you deserve: number one, 'Don't play with matches,' and number two, 'Look both ways before crossing the street.' "

Marvin said, "Oh, man! That talking book is the bomb! The insults I'm gonna learn once I get my hands on it!"

Russell whispered to Steven, "We gotta watch out for him, Bucko, something tells me he's a crook."

Steven whispered back, "Don't worry, Russell. I'll protect this dictionary with my life." And to show how serious he was he raised his right hand.

Richelle said, "All right, all right. It is so rude to whisper, knock it off and let's go find out what our next mission is."

She knocked on Mr. Chickee's door.

Ms. Tiptip answered and relief swept over her face.

"Finally! Come in, come in. We've been so worried."

She hugged the Flint Future Detectives. Steven and Russell made funny faces at each other.

The sullen guide saw Ms. Tiptip and skulked off the porch. He hollered to Richelle, "I'll wait out here. Get my pay and be snappy about it."

The three friends followed Ms. Tiptip into Mr. Chickee's living room.

She called out, "Othello, it's them! They're all safe!"

Mr. Chickee set down a newspaper. "Oh, thank goodness! I'm so happy you're safe, but do you have the Munchker?"

Russell reached back in his front shirt pocket.

Ms. Tiptip said, "Othello! You were right! They *are* marvelous!"

Richelle said, "Mr. Chickee, Ms. Tiptip, we didn't think that was going to take anywhere *near* that long! I'm afraid we might run out of time, we have to get started on the next mission right away."

"You're right, Richelle. Let me turn on the Holo-Vision."

He said, "Russell, please move that newspaper for me."

Russell picked up Mr. Chickee's paper. He read the headline: NEW SUPER-GIGANTIC NUMBER DISCOVERED; CALLED A "BRAZILIAN." FOUND TO BE SAME SIZE AS A HUNDRED SKILLION.

Russell threw the paper on the floor. Mr. Chickee raised his hands to clap but Russell beat him to the punch.

Horton Flum-Flub Holo-Explainer appeared on the middle of the table. He bowed and said, "Welcome, one and all." (But guess who he didn't look at!)

He bowed in Russell's direction and said, "Congratulations on successfully completing the first mission, Russell Braithewaite Woods. In honor of your accomplishment I have been asked to compose a poem. It has been placed in the Ourside Archives of Heroes. Please allow me to repeat it."

Russell said, "Wow. Great! That's so coo—"

Horton said, "Sorry to interrupt, but we're on a pretty tight schedule here. All I really need is your permission."

Russell said, "Oops! You can do it!"

Horton closed his tiny holographic eyes, cleared his throat, then flung his arms wide open.

> *"Why? You got me.*
> *Where? No idea.*
> *When? Beats me.*
> *But will rainbows care?"*

Horton bowed again and waited in that embarrassing way people do when they're expecting you to clap for them. Everybody did.

"Thank you! Thank you! Really, you're much too kind!"

Steven started to say, "Huh? I—"

But Ms. Tiptip put her hand on his arm and said, "Horton, once again you've proven there is no other person who can do to a poem what you do. Now these fine people need to know where their next mission will take place."

Horton disappeared and a map of Ourside filled the table.

Richelle said, "There! I just had a feeling in my gut that I need to go there."

Russell said, "Don't be so sure, Madam President, some of the time those feelings are nothing but diarrhea."

Richelle said, "Russell! Be quiet. It's right there, Ms. Tiptip."

Richelle touched a place on the table that looked like a giant city with a bright blue dot in the middle of it.

Mr. Chickee and Ms. Tiptip smiled.

He said, "Boys, it looks like you and I will be hanging out for a while."

Ms. Tiptip said, "Richelle, good news, I'll be accompanying you there. There will be no need to hire a guide!"

Steven slapped his forehead and said, "The guide! I just about forgot, we have to pay him."

Ms. Tiptip handed Steven an envelope. "That's payment in full. Richelle, we need to get started, this is another mission that might prove to have a few surprises in it."

Ms. Tiptip walked to the door. The Flint Future Detectives followed her.

She gave Mr. Chickee a hug.

"Be safe, Naomi."

"I think you might have a harder time with these two than I will with Richelle."

They smiled.

Ms. Tiptip walked onto the porch. "Come, my dear, the next porch is right next door."

Steven and Russell followed them onto Mr. Chickee's porch.

Richelle and Ms. Tiptip walked to the porch next door, turned to wave, then opened the door.

"Pssst!"

Steven turned around. On the side of the porch Marvin Surly-Guide suddenly appeared.

"Well?"

Steven handed him the envelope.

The teenager said, "Thanks for nothing."

He started to leave but said to Steven, "Don't think it wasn't fun, but you see, you guys and me could never hang."

Russell said, "Why not?"

Marvin said, "Well, for starters, look at him." He pointed at the front of Steven's shirt.

"You think I'd hang out with someone who spills food all over their shirt like that?"

Steven looked down and said, "What food?"

Man! If you think Buster B. Bayliss fell for the second-oldest trick in the world, Steven had just fallen for the absolute oldest one. As soon as he looked down, Marvin took his finger and boinged Steven in the nose and said, "Psych!"

Rodney Rodent began whining in Russell's pocket.

Marvin jumped off the porch, ran into the woods by Mr. Chickee's house and said, "You think I'd hang with someone who'd fall for that? Fat chance, chump!"

Then he disappeared in a thick grove of trees.

Rodney Rodent was becoming so rambunctious and whiny that Russell had to take him out of his pocket.

"What, Rod-Rode? What's wrong? I couldn't hear you."

Rodney Rodent sounded very disappointed, "Big buddy! The words I said were very clear, I can't believe this happened. Don't look now but that rotten kid your talking book's kidnapped! Call nine-one-one, call Mr. C., you're gonna need advice. If Bucko goes off by himself, the ree-sult won't be nice!"

Russell looked around Steven's neck, and sure enough

Great-great-grampa Carter's dictionary was gone; only the cord hung around Steven's neck.

Russell knew he had to follow Rodney's advice. He yelled, "Mr. Chickee!"

Their friend walked out onto the porch.

"Yes, Russell?"

"I hate to burp Bucko's bubble, but that kid just stole his dictionary!"

Steven put his hand to his neck and felt the dangling cord. "What?"

He started off the porch in the direction Marvin had disappeared.

Mr. Chickee called, "Steven! Stop! We can't possibly know which direction he took. We can't do anything until Ms. Tiptip and Richelle come back. We'll have to wait."

Steven said, "I *can't* wait, Mr. Chickee! That's part of my family history!"

"I know, Steven, but there's nothing more to do, we simply have to wait."

Steven said, "When I get my hands on that thief, he'll wish he hadn't messed with the presid—the *former* president of the Flint Future Detectives!"

Mr. Chickee said, "Patience, Steven, patience. Once people from the Guide family go bad, they go very bad. We'll have to carefully consider our next move. This has the smell of a danger rating of nine and a half. I promise you, once the women are safely back and we've set out on the final mission, we'll get to the bottom of this."

Rodney Rodent whined to Russell, "Big buddy! Mr. Chickee's right, he speaks the truth, there's nothing more to do. Tell Bucko that he'll meet that thief before his mission's through. Big troubles, woe and tons of pain Bucko will have to see, before he gets that mean book back, before it's finally free. Tell him this, to keep in mind what my mummy used to say: The best-laid plans of Munchkers and men will often go astray."

Steven looked at his Oops-a-Daisy.

Russell looked at his Oops-a-Daisy.

Mr. Chickee looked at the sky.

Rodney Rodent looked at the woods.

Each was thinking the same thing: "This is turning out a lot worse than I ever imagined!"

And if they thought their adventure was going to be over soon, I'm sorry 'bout their luck!

About the Author

CHRISTOPHER PAUL CURTIS is the bestselling author of *Bud, Not Buddy*, winner of the Newbery Medal and the Coretta Scott King Medal, among many other honors, and most recently of *Mr. Chickee's Funny Money* (a companion to *Mr. Chickee's Messy Mission*) and *Bucking the Sarge*. His first novel, *The Watsons Go to Birmingham—1963*, was also singled out for many awards, among them a Newbery Honor and a Coretta Scott King Honor. Christopher Paul Curtis grew up in Flint, Michigan. After high school, he began working on the assembly line at Fisher Body Flint Plant No. 1 while attending the Flint branch of the University of Michigan, where he began writing essays and fiction. He is now a full-time writer.